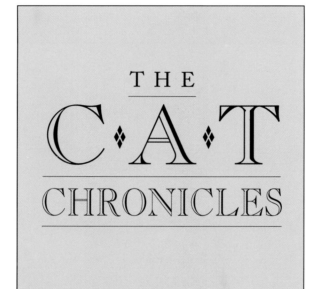

THE
C·A·T
CHRONICLES

THE
C·A·T
CHRONICLES

One cat...nine adventurous lives...
Each lived in a different time and place

TOM HOWARD

RUNNING PRESS
PHILADELPHIA PENNSYLVANIA

A Quarto Book

Copyright © 1993 Quarto Inc

All rights reserved under the Pan-American and International Copyright Convention. No part of this publication may be reproduced, stored in a retrieval system or transmitted in any form or by any means electronic, mechanical, photocopying, recording or otherwise, without written permission of the publisher and copyright holders.

9 8 7 6 5 4 3 2 1

Digit on the right indicates the number of this printing.

Library of Congress Cataloging-in-Publication Number 93-83534

ISBN: 1-56138-291-4

This book was designed and produced by
Quarto Inc
The Old Brewery, 6 Blundell Street
London N7 9BH

Senior Editor: Honor Head
Senior Art Editor: Penny Cobb
Publishing Director: Janet Slingsby
Art Director: Moira Clinch
Designer: Terry Jeavons
Illustrators: Alan Baker *(main story illustrations)*
Marion Appleton *(margin illustrations)*
Ruth Grewcock *(borders)*
Picture Manager: Rebecca Horsewood
Picture Research: Anne-Marie Ehrlich

Typeset in the UK
Manufactured in Singapore by Eray Scan
Printed in Hong Kong by Leefung-Asco Printers Limited

This book may be ordered by mail from the publisher. Please add $2.50 for postage and handling. *But try your bookstore first!*

First published in the USA in 1993 by
Running Press Book Publishers
125 South Twenty-second Street
Philadelphia, Pennsylvania 19103-4399

CONTENTS

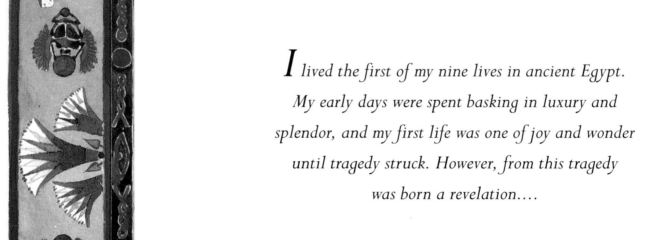

I lived the first of my nine lives in ancient Egypt.
My early days were spent basking in luxury and
splendor, and my first life was one of joy and wonder
until tragedy struck. However, from this tragedy
was born a revelation....

1

THE
ARCHITECT'S
CAT

My home was the house of Imhotep, a sculptor and the Pharaoh's architect and engineer: a place of cool halls, gardens full of flowers, palm-shaded walks, and pools of sparkling water. I could bask in the sun or rest in the dappled shade, hunt for frogs or chase butterflies as I wished.

Mother had told me "Your father is one of the temple cats at Bubastis. I slipped away and met him when Imhotep took me to the temple of the great goddess Bast."

I was lucky enough to inherit the true look of the Goddess's own Mau cats, the long sleek body and the compact, yet finely crafted head, ending in the exquisite tips of the pointed ears. And mother had brought me up with an understanding of the duties, as well as the rare privileges that go

with the honor of being born with the sacred blood of Bubastis.

It was a comfortable life. There was no need to lift a paw. Fresh fish was brought to me daily from the Nile, caught by my own slave Mio, whose duty was to attend to my every whim — though I made few demands on her. The human family often invited me to join in their banquets; I sat beneath the chair of Imhotep's wife, where she would slip me special delicacies from the feast. My mother supervised my rearing and education; from her I learned my duties as a cat of Bast. She was an indulgent parent, and since I was her only surviving kitten, had the leisure to teach many of my lessons through play. Even in the heat of the day, she would twitch her tail for me to chase.

Often she was called to pose for Imhotep. He would model her statuette: to be cast in bronze as a votive offering for the temple, to embellish the household of the Pharaoh or one of his nobles, or to be glazed and fired in a kiln to make a faience figurine for a lesser offering or talisman. She was the picture of feline beauty; serene and graceful, she could sit completely still for hours, unlike her impatient kitten. I doubt that I managed even half her degree of elegance when it was my turn to become the sculptor's model.

Later, when my mother was no longer with us, I would lie in the lap of the architect as he rested after working all day for the Pharaoh. I watched him playing with counters on a board. I sometimes felt a temptation to and knock one to the floor, but I resisted; enough that through me the goddess bestowed good luck upon his game.

My closest human companion was Imhotep's little daughter, Sekhmet – though anyone less like the fierce lion-goddess for whom she was named it is impossible to imagine. The earliest memory I have, curled up against my mother's warmth when my eyes had hardly opened, was little Sekhmet smiling down at me and laughing her tinkling laugh. "How beautiful she is. Her fur is so soft – like touching silk," she said. I thought her very pretty, too. She always seemed to be there, laughing as I sucked my mother's milk or sympathizing as I was subjected to a thorough washing from the sandpaper side of mother's tongue. It was Sekhmet who called me Pasht, or Puss, after my goddess's other name. Soon it was Sekhmet who was calling the slave, "Bring food for my hungry Pasht," or snatching the brush from the slave's hand, saying, "Too rough! Too rough!" and stroking my fur with her own gentle hand to make it smooth and shiny.

We invented many games together: chasing and pouncing trailing, tasseled cords, running after balls of stitched cloth stuffed with straw. I would retrieve items she hid or threw, finding them by scent, or by listening carefully to identify where they fell. Often we played hide and seek together. I had the advantage, for her nose and ears lacked the sensitivity we cats possess, and being so much smaller, it was easier for me to hide. Often I had to meow or pop my head out from the hiding place, or she would never have found me.

One day, when I was nearly fully grown, Sekhmet was taking her afternoon siesta in a hammock slung between two palm trees by the pool. I climbed up onto the roof of one of the garden shelters to investigate a bird's nest while there was no one to reprove me for my interest in the fledglings – Sekhmet had become very upset and scolded me when I once brought her a young bird as a present. I had just closed in far enough to see that there were two youngsters in the nest when suddenly all the birds in the garden squawked in unison. Then I heard my mother's voice sending out a signal to beware. She sounded agitated and urgent. However, it was not my presence all these voices warned of, but a far greater danger lurking in the garden.

With all the birds distracted by this commotion, I could have snatched a chick with ease, but my mother's signal put all else out of my mind. The great enemy in the garden was – Apep's animal. Every morning, mother had taught me, the great god Ra takes the form of a cat to fight Apep, the serpent of the night who swallows the sun to bring the dark. Only Ra's victory prevents the sun from being swallowed forever and heralds the dawn.

Not all snakes are harmful. There are some that protect the Pharaoh and his kingdom – represented in the design of the Pharaonic crown – and other households welcome their own house-snake to help keep down rats and vermin and to discourage other snakes. However, which can you trust? Until then, I had never seen a real snake, either good or bad. As a young cat, I had been warned to avoid them; even a good snake might mistake a playful kitten for a scampering rat.

At my mother's signal, I was momentarily too shocked to move, then I rushed to the edge of the roof to survey the scene below. It was not difficult to deduce where the enemy was: by the concentration of warning calls, by the direction in which the frogs were jumping, and most clearly by the movements of the leaves as the enemy made its

11

sinuous way among the plants — and it was moving fast. Then I saw it, zigzagging out onto the path beside the pool. I had expected it to be much larger — for surely Apep must be huge to swallow the sun ship every night. Why should this thing be considered so dangerous? I could easily handle this poisonous serpent myself. Mother must have seen me about to leap down off the roof, for she called out, "Leave it!" How I wish that I had obeyed her command.

The snake moved along the poolside and past the fountain to the flower-decked arbor where little Sekhmet slept. Where was her slave? Why didn't the humans come to her rescue? Couldn't they hear the warning calls? And where was mother? Why didn't she pounce? I knew she must be waiting in ambush, but it would soon be too late. I froze in horror as the snake began to coil around the trunk of one of the palm trees and creep toward Sekhmet. My playmate was in danger. I must stop this from happening. I forgot everything I had learned about how to stalk and hunt. I rushed to Sekhmet's rescue.

In a whisker's twitch, I reached the foot of the palm tree, but the killer was already way above me, his head twisting down the hammock cords. Scrambling up the trunk I pursued him, but only managed to drag my claws along the end of his disappearing tail. At that moment a slight tremor in the branches above me revealed my mother leaping down. She had been in ambush waiting for the precise moment to attack. Her timing was perfect, but my attempt to attack the snake had drawn him back, in that split second making mother miss the precise spot behind the head to inflict a fatal bite. She struck too low, and his fangs caught a rear paw.

How she maintained her balance was a miracle; the goddess must have been with her. Their battle shook the hammock and woke Sekhmet, who screamed for help and jumped down to safety. I feinted around the snake to distract him. He ignored me, so I took my chance and made the killing bite myself.

At last a slave came running with a knife and hacked off the serpent's head. He then began to suck the poison from my mother's wound, spitting out each mouthful. It was too late. The poison was already pulsing through her body, and I nuzzled her helplessly as her life ebbed away.

Imhotep was sent for. Hugging his crying and trembling daughter to him, he gave an emotional prayer of thanks to the goddess Bast. "Oh, thank you, most sacred one, for delivering my youngest child from the arms of death, by sending your servant to save her." Then he knelt beside mother and gave the orders for due honor and ceremony to be shown. Her favorite cushion was brought, and she was gently lifted and carried into the house. I wanted to follow, but Sekhmet picked me up in her gentle hands to comfort me.

The embalmers came, and mother was given over to them to prepare her for her journey to the gods. The family and all the household mourned her, shaving off their eyebrows in an outward display of their grief. When at last the embalmers brought her back to us, she was greeted with shaking metal rattles and wailing songs which sounded like our own cat music. To this, I added my own sad voice. My brave mother had been wrapped in bandages which were interwoven in the pattern of her fur, with colored stones placed to represent her eyes. I knew mother was underneath, for I could smell her through the bandages, but there were other odors, too, strange smells I could not identify: the scent of exotic flowers and perfumed oils. Opposite her was placed the finest of the bronze figures that Imhotep had made of her. When everyone had honored my mother's spirit, she was placed within a case, beautifully modeled from papyrus pulp and painted in her likeness. Sekhmet attached a cord to the collar around my neck, and we set out for the temple.

My mother's corpse traveled in the first litter, carried reverently on Imhotep's lap, and I traveled in the second with Sekhmet. The journey was long, and emotionally exhausted, I curled up on Sekhmet's lap and fell asleep. She woke me gently when we stopped outside the temple and lifted me down to the ground.

The temple gates were huge, and the walls seemed to extend to the sky. I called to Sekhmet, and she lifted me to her shoulders so that I could see everything more clearly.

We passed through halls adorned with huge figures carved on every side, eventually arriving at an inner garden. There Imhotep handed a bag of silver to a priest sitting within a low-walled enclosure where the temple cats were sunning themselves. The priest placed the silver on the scales and measured out an equal amount of fresh Nile fish for the temple cats. Then another priest led us into the presence of Bast herself. The goddess sat on a high throne and had a body almost like a woman, but with the most beautiful cat's head. With great reverence, Imhotep handed my mother's body to the priest who spoke the ritual welcome and turned with her to face Bast.

I felt an overwhelming urge to be beside my mother one last time. Sekhmet had loosened her hold on me, and on a sudden impulse I jumped from her shoulder. She tried to run after me, but the priest stopped her. I leaped onto the lap of Bast and, purring, rubbed myself against her. She felt cold. This was not the goddess herself but an image; yet, as my fur rubbed against her, I thought I heard an answering purr and felt the stone grow warm. The great goddess had made her presence felt to comfort me in my sorrow. In that moment, I knew that I could leave mother safely in her care.

Jumping down, I crouched for a moment before mother in her casket. I said goodbye, knowing we would meet again when I eventually made the same journey. Then I walked back to Sekhmet and turned back to face the goddess. Her deep, fathomless eyes seemed to look straight into mine, and I felt an inner strength and sense of purpose surge through me that I knew would be with me for the rest of my life. Now I was ready to take over from my mother.

I stayed with Sekhmet as she grew to womanhood, and after her marriage, raised my own family at her new home. Although I never returned to the temple, the memory of my visit on that sad day stayed with me always. Life has no terrors for me now. I know that I have the protection of the goddess, and that when my time comes I will find her waiting to welcome me.

THE ARCHITECT'S CAT

This cat lives in ancient Egypt, during the 22nd Dynasty (945–712 B.C.) at a time when the goddess Bastet (also known as Bast) became important throughout Egypt.

The cat, along with many other animals, such as the falcon, ibis, baboon, crocodile, and hippopotamus, was linked with Egyptian gods. All had to be treated with respect. When a family's pet cat died, the whole household went into mourning.

Bubastis Temple

Bubastis, at the head of the Nile Delta, was the cult center for the worship of Bastet. Each year, pilgrims from all over Egypt came to a great festival. The temple, which was surrounded by tree-lined canals, was originally dedicated to Bastet as the lioness of the sun 4,500 years ago. Bastet, later depicted with the head of a cat, was worshipped throughout ancient Egypt, especially after Bubastis became its capital.

Mummification

Cat mummification was not as elaborate as that performed on people. Natron, a naturally occurring compound of sodium carbonate and sodium bicarbonate, was used to dehydrate and preserve the body. When this process was complete, the cat was usually arranged in a sitting posture before being wound in a sheet of linen and then closely bandaged.

Punishable by death

Harming a cat was anathema to the ancient Egyptians. According to Greek and Roman reports in the classical period, killing a cat deliberately might be punishable by death. A Roman diplomat who accidentally killed a cat nearly got lynched by an Egyptian crowd. Persian soldiers attacking an Egyptian city in 525 B.C. are said to have carried cats, and the Egyptian soldiers surrendered rather than risk harming the cats.

Owners mourned the death of a cat by shaving off their eyebrows as a mark of respect.

Fertility goddess

There is a painting of a cat in a tomb at Beni Hassan from about 4,000 years ago. Several Theban tombs dating from about 600 years later show cats in domestic situations, sitting on laps or under chairs. One, in which the cat wears a collar and leash, must be a pet, and cats seem by then to have become an accepted part of palace and domestic life. Their depiction under chairs, always those of women, may be symbolic and intended to represent female fertility, for Bastet is a fertility goddess. Another Theban painting shows the sculptor Nebumun apparently hunting in the marshes of the delta with a throwing stick. It is often suggested that the cat in this picture is being used as a retriever. Some cats will play retrieving games, and they can certainly carry quite large birds and rabbits in their jaws. However, the cat in this picture, too, may be symbolic, representing the fertility of the delta and reassuring the dead of plenty in the afterlife.

Domestication

The wild species of cat from which the domestic cat developed is the African form of the Wildcat *Felis sylvestris lybica*, perhaps with some hybridization from the Jungle Cat *Felis chaus*. The first firm evidence of domestication comes from Egypt. However, whether cat scavengers acclimated to humans and became pets or if wild cats were caught and kept in temples where their kittens were gradually domesticated remains a matter of conjecture.

The modern breed of the Egyptian Mau, recognized by the American Cat Fanciers in 1968, looks very like some of the ancient Egyptian paintings of cats. It was developed from cats found on the streets of Cairo, and it might be claimed to be a direct descendant of the ancient cats. Rather oriental in appearance, but with a somewhat heavier body, it has a spotted coat with tabby-like stripes on the face, and an "M"-shape on the forehead. The legs and tail are barred and ringed.

British breeders set out to create a very similar type from tabby-marked Siamese. The British registration body would not accept the name Mau, and their breed is known as the Oriental Spotted Tabby.

The cat of Ra

The ancient Egyptian sun god Ra takes cat form to slay the serpent of darkness, which each night swallows the ship which carries the sun through the heavens. This victory of Ra over the serpent must be repeated every morning to guarantee the coming of the new day.

It was said that the glittering eyes of a cat at night represented the continued existence of the sun during the nighttime hours.

The ceremony of Bastet

Many figures of Bastet show her carrying an aegis, a ceremonial basket shield, and a sistrum, a musical instrument with moving rods which is shaken to make a metallic rattling and used in the worship of Isis. Often she has a group of cats or kittens at her feet. It is believed that the word "puss" may be derived from the name Bast.

The Bayer–Anderson Cat

One of the most beautiful of all Egyptian cat figures, known as the Bayer–Anderson cat after the donors who presented it to the British Museum, wears gold earrings and has a scarab, the sacred beetle, inscribed on its chest.

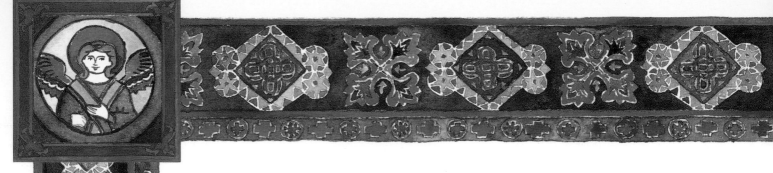

My second life began in the humble surroundings
of a twelfth-century barn — and nearly ended
before I reached full cathood. But I was plucked from
death's door by a kindly monk who showed me a
different way of life....

2

THE
MONK'S
CAT

My new life began in the byre behind a small village house near the river bank. I don't remember much about the early part of it except romping with my siblings in the straw and the lessons in mousing that our mother gave us. If we roamed even as far as the shed door, our over-protective parent would agitatedly call us back to her side. "Be careful of the goats and cows!" she would warn. "They might trample you." As if any of us was so slow that we could not dodge their ambling hooves! It was just as well that I was a disobedient kitten because, ironically, my heedless, inquisitive nature saved my life.

I awoke suddenly in the middle of a dark, moonless night, wondering what had disturbed my sleep: it surely must be something unusual, as familiar sounds would never wake me. I strained every sense, but I could hear only the breathing of the other kittens curled around me, the movement of the cattle in the straw, and the sighing of the wind. Then I heard a human moving. There was nothing unusual in that, even in the middle of the night. From time to time, someone would step outside their cottage to relieve themselves or to keep a romantic assignation in the night — in this respect humans are not so different from cats. But something was amiss. The sounds were made by several pairs of footsteps, which were uncertain, as if unfamiliar with the geography of the place. I could smell the scent of fear and stealth; these were humans on the hunt.

Careful to extricate myself from the bundle of my brothers and sisters without waking them, I set out to investigate. There was a flickering light beyond the crack in the door, but, as I crossed toward it, the door was flung open and I was knocked back behind it. I hid there as men burst in and drove the cattle out. Now mother was awake and, finding me missing, called me to her; but before I could get back to her, the intruders threw a flaming brand into the byre and the straw between us caught ablaze. In just a few moments, the whole shed was on fire. Mother screamed to me to run and tried to marshall her kittens past the flames. But, with the smoke, the kicking of a panic-stricken goat, and the speed with which the fire spread, they had no chance. Instinct made me dash through the burning straw and out through the door. I ran and ran until only the river was ahead of me.

Not until I stopped did I notice that my fur was smoldering and my tail aflame. Then suddenly I was being lifted up and quickly dipped in and out of the water. That shock was worse than being on fire. What a state I was in; scorched, bedraggled, and sopping. But soon I found myself being patted and rubbed with a rough cloth until I was half-dry again.

The man who had rescued me sat below the ridge of the bank where the light of the flames would not reveal him. He had that same smell of fear, but smelled friendly, too. After I had finished drying my fur with my tongue, I crept into his sleeve to escape the chill of the wind. He was dressed in a heavy monk's habit, and in the warmth and safety of his arms, I fell asleep. While I slept, the murderous pirates who had looted and burned our entire village sailed off, taking with them cattle they had slaughtered and the children they had kidnapped to be their slaves.

I think the monk slept, too, and dawn woke us both. The horrors of the night came flooding back to me, and I ran back to the charred embers of home, frantically calling for mother. It was no use; the cottage was a ruin. The people of the village were sifting through the burnt remains of their homes to salvage what they could of their possessions. They had no time for a tired and hungry kitten and shoo'd me away. There was no comfort to be had here, and when the monk picked me up murmuring, "There, there...." and stroked me, I gratefully sank into his arms. A new stage in my life had started.

My new home was the monastery on the hill above the village. The raiders had ransacked the monastery, too, and they had set the wooden outbuildings ablaze. The flames had spread to the roof of the church, but the stone walls stood strong. One of the monks had been brutally murdered as he tried to stop the marauders from taking sacred gold and silver vessels from the altar; another was slain at the foot of the tower as he tried to reach the great bell to raise the alarm. The other brothers were fortunate enough to have escaped into the darkness of the night.

First the monks buried their dead brethren, then held a service for those the village had lost. I mourned my own. I had almost reached the age when I would have left the family nest anyway, so I soon adjusted to my new circumstances. By the time my scorched fur had grown again – and kitten fur grows fast – I had marked out my territory and was settling into monastic life.

My new life had many advantages. The regular pattern of religious ceremonies, day and night, gave a reassuring discipline to life. The stone walls kept out winter winds, and the blanket covering the monk's cot was a comfortable place to sleep when it was cold, the cloister a good place to lie in the sun. The food supply was regular, if basic, although occasional delicacies were available from the Abbot's table when important visitors passed through.

I made my contribution to the monastery chores at planting time, chasing the birds from the fresh-sown ground. I avoided most of the more onerous duties. When I became skilled at catching them, the mice and rats were enough to provide me with sport and keep me fit. There was plenty of time to enjoy life, and I was always on the lookout for new things to investigate. The discovery of catnip in Brother John's herb garden contributed greatly to my hours of outdoor pleasure.

With the help of new brethren sent to join them, including skilled masons and carpenters, the monks began repairing the damage to the church roof. From below I watched them high on the roof ridge, and I longed to be up there with them, able to see out to the limits of my territory and beyond. Early one morning, I decided to climb up there while the monks were at Matins.

Climbing scaffolds and ladders was much more difficult than it looked. The ladders I could manage, where they were in place, but they did not go far enough, and the scaffold poles were so thin they were almost impossible to clamber up. I made my way as high as the top of the windows, but no further. Even from there, the view was amazing, but it was so frustrating not to be able to go farther.

The descent proved to me that, in typical cat fashion, I had been overambitious in going so far up. I slipped and slithered as I tried to back down a pole. The ladder was made of rope and gave no footing — the only thing to do was jump. I shut my eyes and launched out into the void. It seemed an age before I felt the ground shuddering beneath my paws. No bones were broken, but every limb was juddering, so I found a hedge and fell asleep. I awoke to the rustle of leaves as a little field mouse tentatively nosed through the undergrowth in search of food, its whiskers twitching. I was too sleepy to chase it, but felt honor-bound to frighten it by making a half-hearted leap at it. Its startled squeak sent other creatures scampering for cover. How I chuckled to myself as I stretched luxuriously.

By now, the sun was high, and the builders were hard at work. I could hear one of them making that wailing noise that they call singing. My frustration unabated, I was determined that somehow I would get up on the roof; but I sensed imminent danger. Something dark loomed above me. Could it be an eagle? No, probably it was just a builder. Nevertheless, I cautiously looked up and saw something diving down toward me…

With relief I realized what it was: the leather bucket suspended on a rope over a pulley which the masons used to haul stones and tools up to the rooftop. This was just what I needed! I went over to the man

filling it and rubbed myself against him, meowing to attract his attention. Then I jumped into the bucket.

"No time to play," he said and tipped me out, but I persisted and jumped back in again, then looked upward. "Hurry up, Egbert," came a shout from up above. "Are y'aving trouble?"

"No, Barney," he called, "but I'm sending you a little present." At last, he'd got the idea.

What a surprise Barney got when I leaped out of the bucket! "Well, I'll be …" He remembered where he was just in time.

I ran up to the highest point of the roof above the west end of the church. The view extended beyond the village, downriver as far as the sea and upstream to the source of the river where forests filled the mountainous landscape. From the edge of the parapet, I could see Brother James feeding the pigs and Brother Martin in the orchard collecting apples.

Having taken in the view, I amused myself by inspecting each workman at his task; the carpenters setting the timbers in place, the tiler laying on the upper surface, and the masons replacing damaged stonework. All the builders greeted me in friendly fashion: "Hey, Lucky, come here!" "You enjoying it up here, Lucky?" I was called Lucky on account of my escape from the fire.

When the wind began to freshen, I decided I had seen enough, so I went back to where the pulley was, but the bucket was not there. I meowed to attract Barney's attention and indicated that I wanted to go down to the ground. It took a moment or two before Barney understood me properly. Then he called down and someone on the ground pulled on the rope to haul the bucket, up. I hesitated for a moment before jumping into the bucket. and before I could launch myself, Barney had gently lifted me and placed me in it. "There you go, Lucky," he said.

As long as work continued on the roof, I took a trip up there every day, hauled up in the morning and let down when my inspection was complete. One of the masons carved a sculpture of me in my bucket into the capital of a door column which was part of the new bell tower they erected. The door led to a stair by which I could make my own way up to the top of the building and out on to the roof.

I went on making a roof inspection every morning, weather permitting, as part of my patrol of the whole monastery. My duties involved keeping the mice in check and the vegetable and herb gardens rid of any other vermin. The majority of my hunting missions I carried out at night, when the mice were active.

I became involved in the religious life of the monastery, attending the daily office, sitting among the choir and sometimes adding a descant to the chanting of the monks. My image is still there, carved on the monks' stalls near the seat that I made my own.

My favorite times, however, were those spent in Brother John's carrel – dozing in his lap if I was tired, or sitting by his inkwell watching him copy out manuscripts and painting delicate illuminations. You will find my portrait in some of those small pictures, perhaps sitting by the Virgin's feet in a tableau of the Holy Family. Of all of them, my proudest picture is the one Brother John painted in a bestiary to illustrate the family of cat: it shows me catching an enormous rat. Perhaps he did exaggerate the rat's size a little, but it was the biggest anyone in the monastery had ever seen. It put up quite a battle, but that's another story.

THE MONK'S CAT

This cat lives in the twelfth century in a village not far from the North Sea. Most buildings during this period were wooden, so it was easy to put whole communities to the torch. Only major churches and important castles were likely to be built in stone.

Raiders plundered settlements along both the British and continental European coasts bordering the North Sea.

Domestication

The northern race of the Wildcat, the European Wildcat *Felis sylvestris sylvestris*, can interbreed with the African form and may have contributed to the ancestry of domestic cats, but European Wildcats themselves have only been domesticated in one or two exceptional cases. They can be distinguished from the domestic tabby with similar mackerel or tiger stripes by their generally heavier build and a bushier, more blunt-ended tail.

The tabby pattern forms the basis for all the ticked, spotted, and striped cat coats. It occurs in both long-hair and short-hair breeds and contributes to the pattern of others, as well as being a common pattern of non-pedigree cats.

The blotched tabby pattern, with whorls on the sides of the body, instead of stripes, seems to have developed in Britain many centuries ago and, gradually spread through Europe and to other parts of the world. The places where bigger populations of cats with blotched patterns occur match the pattern of trade routes used by British merchants.

Danger! Raiders!

Attacks by Scandinavian raiders on the British Isles are recorded from 789 A.D. The first was mistaken for a trading expedition until the "merchants" killed the

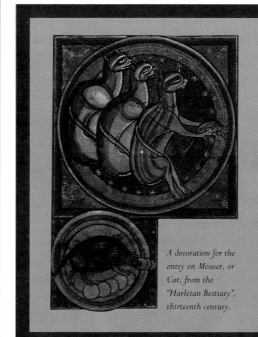

A decoration for the entry on Mouser, or Cat, from the "Harleian Bestiary", thirteenth century.

Fantastic

Bestiaries were medieval natural history books displaying the variety of God's creation. They were based on an original ancient Greek text, but over the centuries many changes and additions introduced fanciful creatures or totally imaginary behavior. The monks copied on trust. Textual authority meant more to scholars than actual observation, so distortions were repeated and exaggerated as they were copied over again.

Fresco of Abbey of
Monteoliveto Maggiore Siena
*by Sodoma shows St. Benedict and
his monks with the monastery pets*

magistrate who went out to
meet them. Although some
were genuine traders,
many lived by looting and
capturing people to make
them slaves.

It was not only coastal
towns that were in danger;
the raiders often penetrated
far up rivers. Raiders from
Denmark sailed up the
Seine, several times

attacking Paris, to which
they laid siege in 885-6 A.D.

In the ninth century, the
raiders sometimes became
colonists, such as those who
invaded eastern British
coasts, moving in-land until
halted by Alfred the Great.
Saxons later paid them
"Dangeld" in return for not
attacking further.

The monks' day

Monks had to attend
services in the abbey church
at intervals through the day
and had to get up during

the night as well. The eight
"Offices" to be said are
spread through the twenty-
four hours. First was
Matins, which theoretically
was celebrated at midnight,
though often postponed
until two or three in the
morning, and this was
followed by Lauds. After a
few hours' sleep, monks
were wakened for the dawn
service, Prime. Three
hours after sunrise was
Terce, at midday Sexts, in
the afternoon Nones and
Vespers, and finally
Compline. Around these
individual prayers,
meditation, penances,
meals, work, and sleep had
to be fitted.

Misericordes

Monks were supposed to
stand through the long
night services. As a
concession, small
ledges were often
placed on the under-
side of choir stalls on
which the monks
could prop them-
selves without
actually sitting down.
They were known as
misericordes because
they showed pity on
the monks, and the
brackets supporting
them were often
carved with work

scenes, allegories, animals,
or figures from fable.

Companions

One pet cat was the only
companion permitted to
the female hermits
belonging to one monastic
order, and cats must have
been familiar residents in
monasteries where the
kitchen would have been a
continuing source of food.

An Irish monk, working
as a scribe in the eighth or
ninth century at a
monastery in Austria,

*Misericorde from Hereford
Cathedral, England.*

wrote a poem des-
cribing his companion
Pangur Bán (White
Cat) and compared his
stint at the copying
desk with the cat's work
keeping down the mice.

Pangur Bán

*I and Pangur Bán my cat
'Tis a like task we are at
Hunting mice is his delight
Hunting words I sit all night*

*Better far than praise of men
'Tis to sit with book and pen;
Pangur bears me no ill-will
He too plies his simple skill.*

A life's work

Before the invention of
printing, all books had to be
laboriously copied out by
hand and each illustration
individually painted. Many
monks were occupied in
this work, sometimes
working with others in a
scriptorium or perhaps in
an individual carrel, or
compartment. Specialists
would paint illuminated
capital letters, concentrate
on figures, or fill in
complex decorative
backgrounds.

*An illuminated manuscript page
from the 15th century.*

I shudder at the thought of my third life, when my friends and I had to endure despair and pain. But this was the early sixteenth century when intolerance and fear were rife. This was not a good time to be a cat, especially a black cat....

3

THE
WITCH'S
CAT

I don't remember much about my kittenhood, except that I often felt inclined to hide. As for my later life, it is painful to recall. Nevertheless I will tell my story.

The farm folk where I was raised seemed to tolerate cats only in their barns, certainly not in their houses. We would patrol around the barns to keep the rodents down. We, in turn, were terrorized by the village boys, who would throw stones at us, or a lot worse if they managed to catch one of us. The best territories around the farm were taken by older cats. For a young tom, it was a meager existence, largely maintained by scavenging.

With good night vision for hunting, my black fur as camouflage, and quick wits to escape danger, I scraped a living for my first year, but my second winter was severe. Pickings were meager; I had to take risks, and I took one too many. Early one morning, I found a dead rabbit caught in a trap. What luck! It still smelled fresh, and I had gotten there before any other hunter. In my haste to get some meat inside me, I reached out to turn the rabbit over and – "wheek"!

The rabbit had not been caught in the trap. It was the bait. If my reactions had not been so fast, the closing trap would have broken my neck. As it was, it only caught my paw. I was lucky. It had not snapped the bone, but the sharp, serrated metal had bitten painfully into the flesh. I pulled to try to free it, but only increased the pressure on the wound. I had to calm myself and think this out.

Should I chew off my paw to free it? No, I must put such drastic remedies to the back of my mind. It was then that I remembered how hungry I was. The rabbit, after all, was already dead, so I sniffed deeply to be sure that there was no greater predator nearby who might seize me as

I had tried to seize the rabbit, and finding that the coast was clear, I gratefully partook of the only meat I had had for days. Despite the gruesome circumstances, this first meal after so long without food tasted good and provided me with strength and stamina.

I was still eating when I heard a human coming and smelled it to be a woman. She came into view, and I saw her break some twigs of mistletoe from an oak tree. I kept absolutely still hoping she might not notice me. But, alas, she came straight toward me.

As she bent over me, I got ready to defend myself, but she did not strike me. Instead, she gripped the skin on the back of my neck just the way my mother would have done to pick me up, and she murmured soft sounds of comfort.

"Poor little mite, you must've bin hungry to steal from a trap wi'out seeing it was sprung. That paw must be painful."

Her hand was reassuring. I let myself relax.

"Now. Let me see what I can do."

Deftly inserting her walking staff between the teeth of the trap in a space beside the rabbit's body, she managed to prize it very slightly open, instantly pulling me backward so that my paw was freed. Now was the time for me to run and hide, but still she held me.

"No, no. Don't try to run away my little one. That paw needs healin'. You shouldn't walk on it."

I wasn't used to humans, so I did not understand the words she said, but some instinct told me her meaning. I felt I could trust her. She lifted me gently, placing me in the folds of her gabardine where it was warm. With one hand she caressed my head. I, in turn, took her finger between my teeth, and she did not attempt to withdraw it, so I nuzzled up to her, forgetting my pain.

It felt strange at first being carried in this way, not at all like swinging from a parent's mouth, but I soon got used to the rocking,

bouncing movement. It was not long before she lifted me out, and I found myself placed gently on a soft cloth in the corner of a small room. There was a fire burning brightly in the hearth, over which a pot was hanging. Along one wall were shelves with many jars and pots of herbs, as well as an array of potions or salves made from them. Bundles of other plants hung drying from the beams.

As soon as I had got my bearings, I began to wash my wound. But scraping my rasping tongue against the raw flesh hurt.

"Now, let's have a look at that paw," the woman said.

She tore up a cloth, ladled some hot water into a bowl, and began to bathe my paw, all the time speaking softly to me.

"Well, Puss, this needs a bit of stitchin'. I'll get us a needle an' thread, but don't you fret yourself. I won't hurt you."

She lit a candle and took down some leaves hanging above my head. One by one, she set them alight and held them smoldering near my nose, gently blowing the smoke toward me and away from her. I began to feel drowsy, and soon I was asleep.

When I woke up, I found my wounded paw had been bandaged.

There was a bowl in front of me with warm goat's milk, and the woman offered me small pieces of food in her hand.

For several days she cared for me in this way like a mother. Nor was I the only animal that she looked after. Nestling in a pot of straw was Blackie, a blackbird with a broken wing which she had taken in to nurse back to health. He would wake us every morning with his song. I soon discovered that the woman helped to heal humans, too.

Whenever the townsfolk came knocking at the door, she made sure that we animals were hidden in the shadows. I thought then it was done lest the people should harm us, as I had already seen humans do.

"Goodbody Grout," they would come and ask, "give me a potion for my headache."

"Some of your powder to ease the birth pangs."

"Make me a salve to clear my pimples."

"Help me, Goodbody, my husband has the ague."

Sometimes they asked her to go to their houses to attend a member of the family. Often they brought gifts of food or cloth. Otherwise they would offer a coin or two in return for her help.

Some asked for love potions or hinted at their needs for poisons, demanded lucky talismans, or begged for spells to protect themselves or harm their enemies. To all of these she turned a deaf ear and said she knew nothing of magic, but some had heard her mumble recipes as she made preparations for them, and none believed her.

The day came when Blackie was fully recovered, and he flew out of the door. However, he did not fly far away from the house but stayed nearby. When my paw was healed, I too was encouraged to make this hearth my home, which I did willingly.

Most mornings, Goodbody Grout would be out early looking for the special plants, herbs, and flowers she required. Soon after noon, she would make the trip again to pick those plants which must be gathered in the sun. Much of the day would be spent cooking and mixing the different remedies from plants and earths. Most of her visitors came when it was dusk, and sometimes she would work late into the night preparing medicines.

If she was leaving at dawn, I would occasionally go with her, helping to sniff out herbs, earning the bowl of milk that I would be given on our return. I watched the house and kept the mice and rats down, always leaving one or two surviving and making sure that Goodbody Grout found no evidence of my hunting, for she would have tried to save every one of my victims. At night, when at last she stopped her work, blew out the candle, and let the fire die down, I would often crawl under her blanket so that we could share our body warmth.

For many seasons this happy life continued, until one night my world fell apart. That evening, I saw a crowd of townsfolk gathering outside, opposite the house. They were waiting for the officer of the watch to arrive. When he came, they all surged forward toward our house. There was a great banging at the door. I hid as usual, and Goodbody Grout went to open it. Before she could reach the latch, the door was forced open and the officer pushed in.

"Goodbody Grout," he began, "you must come with me. A deposition has been …"

But his voice was drowned by the shouts from outside.

"Bring her out!"

"Burn the witch!"

"Beware the imps!"

"I be no witch," our Goodbody protested, but they would not listen to her. The men took her out into the night and she made no resistance as she was roughly led away.

I did not know what to do, and stayed, cowering, in my hiding place until they had all gone. Blackie, in the tree outside, was able to fly after them to the town hall, where they locked Goodbody in the cellars. Blackie saw her through a barred opening at ground level.

It emerged that our Goodbody had been accused of causing the still-birth of Mistress Hankin's baby with a posset she had given the mother to ease the labour pains. I thought that the townsfolk whom she had so often helped would make sure that she was released. But no one spoke for her. Instead, old incidents were remembered and blamed upon her. One person charged that she had cast a spell which had made a cow's milk dry up; another claimed she had caused a man to fall from his horse and crack his skull open. It seemed as though Goodbody Grout had become the scapegoat for everyone's problems, and the accusations multiplied.

They kept her imprisoned in the cellar for days. Blackie saw them bring her food and water. She was not guarded but her hands were tied, except when they gave her the food, and the cell was locked. We had to find a way to free her.

I waited until the town was sleeping and all was quiet. Then I set out for the town hall.

When I reached the prison I jumped down between the bars of her cell window. She was delighted to see me; I rubbed against her lovingly but there was no time to spend on showing more affection. I began chewing through the rope that bound her. Blackie managed to get into the town hall and sought out the hook where the key to her cell was hanging — he had already watched carefully through the windows to find out which one it was — and took it in his beak. Many times the heavy iron key proved too weighty for Blackie and he dropped it, but he persisted in trying to bring it to us.

Dawn was breaking when I gnawed through the last strands of the rope. I went out onto the square and back in to the hall, where I found Blackie had got the key halfway down the cellar steps. One blow of my paw knocked it down to the bottom. It was Blackie's task to fly with the key to the grilled opening in the cell door and push it through. It was then we heard the watch returning.

"I hear a Witchfinder arrived and took quarters at the tavern last night," said one guard.

"Aye, he gave orders as to be awakened early so he could see the woman before Justice Greenhelm opens court."

"We'd best see to her now then, so she be ready."

"James lad! The key be gone."

The guards came charging down the stairs. Blackie and I retreated into the shadows but the key could not be hidden.

"It's all right, it's here by the door. I must have dropped it."

As he bent down to pick the key up he must have seen me.

"Hold still, Holy Jesus, there's summat in the corner. Give us your cloak James, quick …"

I made a dash for it and found a way through all the legs on the stairs. In the confusion Blackie also made his escape.

"'Tis one of the devil's imps, come here to free her."

"Heaven protect us! There's a flying spirit, too!"

When they found Goodbody Grout's hands untied, they were certain it had been the work of the devil. Our attempts to free her had provided her persecutors with their strongest evidence.

After a brief confrontation with Goodbody Grout, the Witchfinder spent all morning interrogating witnesses. Then he declared that he was ready for the court.

The Justice duly took his seat at two hours after noon. A succession of people made their accusations, giving evidence that they had seen the Goodbody gathering ingredients for magic mixtures, making potions, muttering spells, and even talking to a toad. They had to be careful to say nothing which would implicate themselves, which was not easy when the herbs had been gathered and the potions mixed at their own request to cure or assuage their ills.

There were several who claimed to have seen Goodbody Grout in communication with a flying devil. Some said it looked like a huge bat, some that it was more like a vulture. Even those who described it as a raven were allowing their superstitious fear to distort Blackie's very ordinary form. As for me, it was bad enough that I was a black cat, though I too was sometimes described as a "huge" and "vicious" creature.

A little girl, an innocent who I remember used to like to pick me up and stroke me, was made to describe how once, when Goodbody Grout was sick, she had returned from an errand for her to find me curled up on the accused's bed, half covered with a blanket. This was construed as evidence that Goodbody Grout had consorted with an evil spirit and like all witches must have shared communion with the devil.

The Justice duly pronounced Goodbody guilty and sentenced her to burn at the stake. The priest came to her cell and urged her to admit her guilt, to declare that she was a witch but now repented, and promised that by so doing she would save her soul for heaven. But the Goodbody steadfastly maintained her innocence.

I did not understand all these things then. Blackie and I only knew that we had failed her. We saw the faggots piled up in the center of the marketplace and sensed the horrors about to occur.

Always, since our attempt to free her, there was an officer stationed outside Goodbody's cell. There was no way we could help her escape now, but I crept back in the darkness anyway. At least I could reassure her that there were some who still cared for her.

Goodbody was lying on a pile of dirty straw when I jumped down into the cell, but she woke up when I nuzzled against her. Sitting with her back to the wall, she took me onto her lap, stroking and cuddling me as I purred and licked her hand. Through the dark hours she talked to me softly so that the guard outside could not hear.

"Tomorrow, they're going to burn me, Puss. Burn me, 'cause I've bin given skills and knowledge that can help and heal. They be good things, not no bad uns. I've used 'em to look after the people in this town and this is the thanks I gets for it. I was never fair of face and no man wanted me for his wife, leastways not one that I would take, and so I've had a solitary life. My friends 'ave bin the wild critters. I cares for all creation, but they thinks me evil. What I learned on my mother's knee goes back through generations of wise women before her, back before knowledge of the Christian God came to these lands. Anyways, we follow his teaching; we help our neighbors.

"But I am an old woman now. My life is nearly over. Better to end it quickly than lie growing weaker and weaker. I regrets I have not passed my learning ,on but the good I'se done cannot be undone."

I think I fell asleep before she did, and we both slept deeply. The next thing I knew, the key was turning in the lock of the cell. Goodbody tried to hide me with her skirt, but it was too late.

The priest held up his cross and called out, "Devil, show thyself!" Then, pointing an accusing finger at me, he shouted to one of the officers, "Throw your cloak over it!"

"In the name of the Heavenly Father, I command that you surrender yourself to His power, that ..."

Smothered by the cloak, I struggled to fight free but could not. My claws caught in the fabric, and it was all I could do to breathe. I got my head free, but they still held me. Then they tied a rope around my neck and another to keep the cloak in place.

The crowd in the square was strangely silent as we were led out from the town hall. First came the Captain of the Watch, then a cleric with a cross, then Goodbody Grout and the priest with her, still muttering his mumbo-jumbo. Members of the Watch marched on either side of them and behind followed the man carrying me, flanked by two more.

I was terrified but what could I do? I tried to show the same composure as Goodbody displayed, walking calmly with her head held high as she mounted the scaffold.

"Behold, the witch!" cried out the Prosecutor. Then he held me up, "Behold, her black cat, an evil spirit which shall burn with her!"

"Burn them! Burn them!" chanted the seething crowd.

They tied Goodbody Grout to a stake in the center of the

scaffold, then cut her hands free. They took the rope around my neck and tied the loose end around hers. Cutting the rope that bound the cloth around me, they pulled it free and threw me into her arms.

"Poor Puss," she murmured, "Why should you suffer, too?"

"Look how she comforts the imp," one townswoman cried.

"When the flames leap, he will claw her," said another.

"Nay, the devils like the flames."

By then, the priest and all the officers had left the scaffold and one brought a torch of fire and set it to the kindling. Soon the flames were all around us and coming nearer. It was not like the hearthfire. There was no smell of singeing of the tail that happened when I lay too close to the embers. But some deeper memory, some older instinct stirred, and my heart beat faster until Goodbody's hand stilled my fear. Blackie flew over us and dropped a bunch of leaves, which landed on my back. The Goodbody put some in her mouth and chewed on them. When they were soft, she put them in mine.

Whether it was the leaves or the smoke billowing around us, I could not tell, but soon I found it hard to breathe and felt myself drifting off long before the heat from the flames caused any pain. The acrid smell of smoke and the jeering cries of the crowd seemed to recede into the distance. I can remember nothing after, just a gentle hand and a soft voice saying, "Puss, dear Puss."

THE WITCH'S CAT

This cat lives in the sixteenth century when a fear of witchcraft began to grow in Europe, and many saw cats as associates of the Devil.

The role of cats in Egyptian religion and other links with pagan belief and heretical sects was probably responsible for the Christian Church associating them with the Devil, especially after 1233 when Pope Clement V declared that heretics worshipped the Devil in the form of a black tomcat.

Cat's eyes glowing in the dark was also responsible for the growing belief that they were demons, as was their ability to turn in mid-fall and thus survive falls from a great height, which would kill or maim another animal or human.

Pottery figure of witch and her cat from Hungary.

Persecution

In 1484 Pope Innocent VIII issued instructions to root out witchcraft and began four centuries of persecution. The Malleus Malleficarum — the "Hammer of Witches" — was published in 1490 by two Dominican monks, the Chief Inquisitors for Germany, as a guide for those who shared their task. Guilt was presumed, scarcely any defense was allowed, and almost anything was permissible as evidence for the prosecution: they thought it better that the innocent should suffer than that the guilty should escape.

Black devil-cats

A cat, especially a black cat, was one form people thought the Devil took. Early in the fourteenth century, the Knights Templar were accused of worshipping him in this form. At places ranging from Metz, in 1344, to Salem, Massachusetts, three and half centuries later, people claimed to have seen black devil-cats. Witches were often accused of having sexual relations with the Devil, sometimes in his cat form.

A cat was also one of the forms into which witches were thought to change themselves At a Scottish witch trial in 1662, the accused even gave the spell she claimed she used to do so. Folk tales from both Europe and America tell of witches seen as cats by people who strike out, wounding them. Then, on the following day, a woman is discovered with injuries identical to those that had been inflicted on the cat.

Cats were also thought of as servants of the Devil. "All cats have a pact with the Devil," declared the French *L'Evangile du Diable* (Devil's Bible). "Their task is to keep watch ... through the night, to see all, to hear all ... the Evil Spirits, warned just in time, always manage to disappear before we can see them."

Witch's servants

In Britain the belief that witches had servants, or familiars, was particularly strong. They might take many shapes. Some were described as being like little dogs, rabbits, reptiles, and other creatures, as well as cats, especially black cats.

Witches were accused of suckling the Devil or his servants on their blood. A woman seen talking to animals might be thought to be a witch, and if she had any warts or cysts on her skin, these were readily identified as places where she had contact with the Devil.

If she let her pet into her bed, she could easily be accused of consorting with the Devil.

Testing time

Tests for a witch included submerging her in water, sometimes strapped in a "ducking stool," a chair on a long arm built for the purpose.

Sometimes the limbs were tied together, the left hand to the right foot and vice-versa. If the "witch" drowned, it showed her innocence; if she survived, then it "proved" that the Devil was helping her!

Another test was to see if she bore the mark of the Devil, a place which was thought to be insensitive to pain, and which might be identified by a mole or any other skin blemish. Such places were pricked with a needle or pointed dagger, or if no such blemishes were discovered, the pricking might continue all over the body until some area which lacked sensitivity was found. It is possible to find parts of the body which can be pricked without pain and perhaps without producing blood, and some investigators even used trick blades which disappeared into the handle of a dagger to guarantee a conviction.

Caricature of King James being haunted by witches as a result of his book.

Royal interest

King James VI of Scotland took a particular interest in witches, having many brought before him for personal interrogation, and wrote a book on the subject called *Daemonology*. When James succeeded to the English crown in 1603, William Shakespeare wrote *Macbeth*, in which witches play an important part, to please him. King James's own study of the subject made him eager to expose false claims of witchcraft, but his interest possibly increased the number of prosecutions.

Witch hunts

There were others who saw the dangers in the witch hunts. John Gaule, an English Puritan Divine, who published a book of sermons on witchcraft in 1646, warned that: "Every old woman with a wrinkled face, a hairy lip, a squint eye, a spindle in her hand, and a cat or dog by her side, is not only suspected but pronounced a witch." It was perhaps less frequent to find a lonely old man being prosecuted as a witch (or warlock as male witches were sometimes called), but there were male victims of the witch hunts, too.

In England and her American colonies, witches were hung, not burned, but in Scotland and continental countries burning, like that of Joan of Arc, was common. In Scotland and continental Europe, torture was officially sanctioned to get a confession. This, it was argued, was for the witch's benefit, for by confessing and repenting a witch could save her or his soul.

Cat persecutions

The Metz cat devil of 1344 was linked to an outbreak of St. Vitus Dance in the town, and for 400 years afterward, its defeat was celebrated by burning 13 cats in an iron cage in the market place. Other places where cats received similar treatment included Paris, where cats were burned on the Feast of St. John, and Ypres, in modern Belgium.

*M*y fourth life as a cat in late sixteenth-century
Turkey was an odd mixture. After an indulged
kittenhood, near disaster, and a long journey, a lucky
encounter enabled me to spend my remaining years
in ease and comfort....

4

THE
CARPET
MAKER'S
CAT

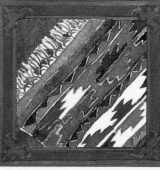

You might not think it, seeing me sitting here in such comfort and splendor, but I started this life as a simple country cat, far from the hubbub of the city. Ahmet was my companion from the beginning. Even when I was a tiny kitten playing with my mother's tail, he was there calling "Sahil, Sahil, let me stroke you," and when I was six weeks old, he took me to live with him.

Ahmet's parents were dead. He lived with his uncle, aunt, and grandmother. They were poor carpet makers who taught Ahmet their skills, and when he was good enough, he began to help them.

They had little enough for themselves, but none of the family made me feel a burden. Perhaps they remembered the cat which used to visit the Prophet Mohammed and in their kindness were following his example. When I first saw the great loom and the balls and hanks of yarn, I thought this a playground made in paradise. As I chased and patted, pounced and snatched, they laughed and did not scold me. But Ahmet sat for many hours undoing the tangles I had made. I was filled with remorse and knew I must not create such havoc again.

Uncle Mustafa saw how diligently Ahmet had put things right and took down a ball of twine from the shelf.

"Here, boy," he said, "a present for your kitten. And try to teach him not to wreck the workshop."

"Did you hear that, Sahil?" Ahmet said, rolling it toward me, "Play with this in future!"

I intended to take his advice, but often found it almost irresistible when watching Aunt Hanife at work. She was faster than all of them, dashing the shuttle of yarn from one side of the loom to the other. Eventually I couldn't resist trying to catch it.

"Look!" she said, "Sahil's trying to help us." I didn't contradict her. I wish I could have helped them with some of their tasks. Anyway, she thanked me by finding an old bobbin and hanging it from the roof-beam on a length of twine where a paw tap could make it swing from side to side or around in circles for me to leap at.

The other village boys would laugh at Ahmet because he gave me as much attention as they did their hunting dogs. Ahmet ignored them. The other boys didn't realize how much fun we had together. They didn't know that I, being an accomplished swimmer, would paddle downstream when Ahmet went fishing in the brook and drive the delicious fish straight into his net. They didn't know how I kept his feet warm at night. They didn't know how I would catch pigeons for him so that we could share a meal.

The seasons passed, and Ahmet grew to manhood. Little changed in our tiny village. Old Granny finally laid down her bobbin and went to heaven; her scolding and her laughter were missed as much as her busy hands and spicy stews. I enjoyed the quiet routine of village life. It's satisfying to know that things will happen when you expect them — and we cats can always find our own excitements. But Ahmet was bored. He had heard travelers' tales of the golden city, Istanbul (Old Byzantium), and he dreamed of going there to seek fame and fortune. Each day he thanked Allah for his blessings and prayed for a chance to leave the village. And destiny decreed it was to happen; though not as Ahmet might have wished.

The dreadful day that changed our lives started like any other. I woke, roused Ahmet, breakfasted, patroled the house to make sure that all was well, then left the family to their carpetmaking and ambled outside to rest in the morning sun.

All morning, it was very still and quiet; but around the time of the midday prayer, I began to feel uneasy. Though nothing tangible gave rise to these feelings, my heart was beating faster than normal.

By the hour of the third prayer, a feeling of general pressure had been joined by an occasional vibration. There were no carts passing by, no people dancing, and this shuddering was quite different from the regular rhythms of the looms. The vibrations became stronger. The ground was shaking, but the humans did not seem to notice.

Perhaps it was my imagination. Strange things can happen to the mind if you spend too long in the sun. But this seemed very real.

Ahmet and Mustafa came out with their prayer rugs, said the ritual words, made their genuflections, and went back to work again. Everything seemed calm, and telling myself to stop worrying, I fell asleep again. I woke in alarm with my paws shaking and raced in to the house to try to tell them that something was wrong. Something awful was going to happen.

"Sahil! No, I can't stop to play now," Ahmet said with a smile "You must wait until work is over."

I felt a stronger tremor. Alarmed now, I tried again, rubbing against Ahmet's legs and then walking toward the door, meowing loudly. He ignored me. I tried the others. I went around the loom and climbed up the half-made carpet screaming at Ahmet through the weft, then at each of them in turn.

"Ahmet, what's wrong with Sahil, has he been taken over by a Djin?" Mustafa said. "Get down! Stop shaking the loom."

"I don't think it's Sahil, uncle…." Ahmet said in a low voice.

Indeed it wasn't. But it was too late. First the lamp toppled, spilling oil which sent a flame across the unfinished carpet, then the walls seemed to move out sideways and the roof crack open; the great beam crashed through the loom, while the floor opened up beneath us. There seemed to be roaring all around. For a moment, the dark room was bright with daylight, and then it was suddenly blacker than it had ever been before.

When I regained consciousness, I was in pitch darkness with a throbbing headache; everything around me was very still and quiet.

Eventually, I heard muffled voices and the sound of shoveling. After a long time, a light began to filter through the blackness. A large boulder was removed, and there seemed to be more space above me. I thought I could squeeze through it. I tried to move. My limbs were all working; neither paws nor tail were trapped.

Somewhere close by I could hear labored breathing. I felt sure it was Ahmet. Sneezing from the dust but trying hard not to dislodge the broken bits of loom and timber or the baked bricks around them, I eased my way through the first space, then smelled Ahmet very strongly. It was his hand. I meowed loudly but got no response, so I gently bit his fingers. He did not answer, but I was glad to find they were warm, with blood still pulsing through them.

Carefully, I maneuvered myself up out of the rubble until I found myself in the fading light of sunset. Above and around me, the scene was chaotic. People were running and shouting, and a boot only just missed my head. Instinctively, I meowed for help.

"It's Sahil! He must have been, buried too. That explains the noise we heard earlier."

There were two men. They were carrying Aunt Hanife.

"Too late, I'm afraid. We've lost both of them."

"There's not much hope for Ahmet. I fear he too will have been crushed by the rubble or suffocated by the dust. I prayed it was him we heard, but it must have been the cat."

Both Hanife and Mustafa were laid upon the ground. They smelled strange and were very cold. They were dead. But I knew Ahmet wasn't. What could I do? I meowed again, and one man bent down to stroke me. I nipped at his sleeve with my teeth and pulled toward the hole I had emerged from. Then rushed over toward it.

"Have you no decency, to want to play at a time like this?" The man was reproachful.

Why couldn't they understand? I began to dig around the hole.

"He's probably just relieved to have escaped entombment, Ali," his friend replied.

At least they were watching me. I went down into the hole, came out again, then went on digging.

"You know, Ahmet used to dote on that animal…Ahmet!

"That's what he's trying to tell us. Fetch lanterns and more help. We must not give up. We could still be in time to save him."

They dug deeply, late into the night, carefully lifting wedged timbers so that the rubble did not collapse and fill the spaces. Ahmet, his loom, and I, had fallen into a chasm beneath the house. Mustafa and Hanife, who had been trapped much higher, were probably choked by the smoke from the smoldering carpets set alight by the lamp. Greater fires had been prevented by the rubble of the upper floors of the house next door which fell above them. At last the diggers reached Ahmet and lifted him gently from the small space he'd lain in for so many hours. He was unconscious but still breathing. I tried to lick the dust off his face; his eyelids flickered open.

Ahmet was nursed in the home of Hassan Bey, the village landowner. He was soon fully recovered, but nothing remained of our home. Though the whole village was badly shaken and many houses had cracks in their walls, the main path of the earthquake had run down our street. Our looms were shattered, the finished carpets burned. All that could be salvaged was Ahmet's own prayer mat. After we had washed it in the stream, it looked as good as new, but that was little compensation for a young man who had lost everything.

Hassan Bey offered us a place in his household, but Ahmet decided now was the time to go in search of fame and fortune. The Bey gave his permission and a gift of three silver pieces. After Ahmet had said his farewells at the graves of his relatives, the whole village came to see him set off. He carried his few possessions in a bag on his back with his prayer mat rolled above it. On the road leading from the village, he picked me up to say goodbye. Didn't he know me better? I was going with him.

We were on the road for many, many days, starting early after the dawn prayer and resting during the heat of the day. When I began to fall behind him, Ahmet would pick me up and put me across his shoulders or on top of his pack.

We would stop only when we found a fresh sparkling stream. Then we would drink, refill Ahmet's flask, and move on.

Often we slept beneath the stars, though we would sometimes

spend the night in comfort at an inn or a caravanserai, where Ahmet would ask to work for his keep and perhaps earn a few coins as well. Given the chance, I would hunt while he slept, not resting until I had fed myself, then dozing half the morning balanced on his bouncing pack like a rider on a camel.

At last we came to the Bosphorus straits. Across the water we could see the Sultan's capital. It was magnificent, the domes of mosques shining in the sun, minarets like fingers pointing up to heaven, and here and there the green of gardens.

It did not look far across the water and I could easily have swum it, but Ahmet took some coins from his savings and gave them to a ferryman, so we were rowed across. It was a strange sensation looking over the side of the boat at the waves all around us, but calm compared with the hubbub which awaited on the farther shore. So many feet, hooves, wheels — and all in such a hurry. I jumped up and found refuge on Ahmet's back, where I had to cling on tightly as we were pushed and jostled by the noisy throng.

I was almost as overwhelmed as Ahmet by the size of the city. My sharp ears were bombarded by so many sounds from all directions and my nose assailed by delicious scents and strange new odors. Stopping several times to ask directions, we eventually found our way to the Street of the Carpet Makers.

It was inside a great bazaar almost as large as a city in itself. We pushed through the crowds along the colonnaded ways. The bazaar was all roofed with arches to protect it from sun and weather, and it was lit at intervals by perforated cupolas. Here wares of every kind were offered for sale, brought from every quarter of the world.

On the Street of the Carpet Makers there stood shop after shop packed with carpets of every color and size, and many more were piled high in storerooms and workshops behind. Here Ahmet hoped to find use for his skills. His mood brightened.

He sought out the most important-looking carpet seller and, pushing his way through the sellers and customers haggling over prices, begged to show his workmanship to the owner. When the shopkeeper agreed, Ahmet unrolled his prayer mat.

"Peasant work," the shopkeeper immediately exclaimed. "It would take years for you to reach my standards. However, if you start at the bottom, I might find you a place. I'll give you your meals, and you may sleep in the shop. If you work hard, after six months I'll reconsider what you're worth."

I knew he was not to be trusted. His glittering eyes showed how highly he prized this carpet, and he smelled of lies. I jumped down onto the prayer mat and stared at him.

"Oh, what a charming pussy!" lisped a portly man who had just walked into the shop as he leant down to stroke me. "And what a lovely carpet. How much is it?"

"It's not for sale," said Ahmet adding, as the man offered a price, "I can't sell it. It's my own prayer mat and the only sample I have of my work."

"You made it? Then roll it up and come to the coffee house with me; we have things to discuss."

We left the shop owner spluttering as we followed the well-dressed stranger out of the shop.

I decided that the stranger was honest. He smelled good – of rosewater and the honey sweetmeats called *loukumi.* I turned my head and purred loudly to signal to Ahmet my approval.

Imagine our astonishment and joy when we learned that this stranger was in charge of buying all the carpets for the Sultan's harem and private apartments within the palace.

He was to become a lifelong friend of ours. It was he who found Ahmet a little house, money for a loom and for colored woolen yarn and bright white cotton; he who gave sound advice on the dangers and delights of the great city. All this was an advance payment for a carpet for the Sultan's harem. When that carpet was completed, another order followed, then more and more. Eventually, Ahmet bought his own shop in the Street of Carpet Makers. He was always busy. Everyone seemed to want his carpets, and he had to take on helpers. Now he has this fine shop in the Great Bazaar, and I am not the only one that shares his life. He has two lovely wives and three handsome sons who show every sign of developing their father's weaving skills. I am a father too, – half the kittens in the bazaar are mine!

Enver, our benefactor, still comes to see us often, taking tea in the back room of the shop or joining us in the coffee house. He always brings a special sweetmeat for me. I am not jealous of Ahmet's new lifestyle, for I still sleep at his feet, and neither wives nor children could ever share as much as I have with the friend whose life I saved and who has been by my side ever since.

THE CARPET MAKER'S CAT

This cat lives in Turkey, in the late sixteenth century. It is a type that probably originated near the shores of Lake Van (after which it is named) in northeast Asian Turkey.

There has been a city on the shores of the Bosphorus for thousands of years. Known first as Byzantium, in 330 B.C. the Emperor Constantine made it the capital of the Roman Empire and changed its name to Constantinople. The eastern part of the Empire survived after Rome fell to the barbarians, and in the sixth century for a time it re-won much of the old Empire. Later centuries saw gradual decline until Constantinople finally fell to Turkish forces in 1453. Extensive building during the rule of Suleyman the Magnificent (1520-66) added new palaces and mosques to what survived of the ancient city.

The covered Bazaar, though rebuilt several times after being destroyed by fire, remains one of the world's great markets. With its own mosques and courtyards, as well as the arcaded streets of shops, it remains a great tourist attraction.

Turkish carpet maker at work

Istanbul skyline

In the swim

The long-haired Turkish Van is very similar in general appearance to the Angora Cat, another breed originating in Turkey. In fact, most of the indigenous Van cats are all white, and local people select kittens with eyes of different colors, one green eye and one blue one.

The western breed of Turkish Van was developed in England from cats with auburn markings on the face and auburn rings on the tail which were discovered by Lake Van in Turkey in 1955. It is often known as "the swimming cat" and native cats do genuinely swim in shallow water along the shore of Lake Van. When they come out of the water, their long fur dries without matting. Most cats will instinctively swim if they find themselves in water, but few will enter it voluntarily. This certainly applies to the Van cats, as to some of the other coastal cats living on the eastern Mediterranean.

Angora cats first appeared in western Europe in the sixteenth century, perhaps before the rather more solidly-built longhairs that we now call Persian cats. It was not until the end of the nineteenth century that much distinction was made between them. Breeders began to prefer the Persian type, and so Angora cats were rarely seen outside Turkey. In 1962, a pair from Ankara Zoo was taken to the United States to re-establish the Angora breed.

Cats and Islam

Respect for other creatures is part of Islamic culture, demonstrated by a story that when a cat fell asleep on the sleeve of his robe, the Prophet Mohammed once cut off a piece of cloth rather than disturb it. One of his close companions was so fond of cats that he was given the name Abu-Khurairha (father of cats).

Raise the alarm

Cats have often been reported giving warning of some danger such as a fire or an earthquake, or of signaling air-raids before the sirens sound.

An animal living more directly by its senses than most people do is more likely to notice signs we miss. Our communication systems through words and language, and our ability to exercise some control over our surroundings, have made it less necessary to be always sensually aware. It is understandable, therefore, that a cat will register the smell and sound of burning or the first tremors of an earthquake before they impinge on human consciousness.

But how does a cat know that enemy airplanes are on the way? Even if they hear them before we do, how do they know that they belong to the enemy?

Any kind of motor has a particular sound and, since airplanes used in World War II made sounds which could be distinguished by the human ear, cats would be able to differentiate between them, too. However, they would also have to learn to associate that particular sound with the actions of going to an air-raid shelter or with some following development which caused them to indicate to their owners that it was time to take cover.

In the same way, there are numerous recorded instances of animals, including cats, leading rescuers to buried or injured people.

Our hero

Simon was the ship's cat on the sloop *Amethyst*, which escaped from the enemy along the Yangtze River during World War II. Although recovering from wounds inflicted by enemy gunfire, Simon was instrumental in making sure that his human companions survived the escape by hunting down and destroying an enemy who had sneaked on board and was threatening the welfare of the humans… Mao Tze Tung, fierce leader of a band of rats, who was raiding food supplies with alarming success. Food was obviously limited and could not easily be replenished, so once Simon had seen off Mao Tze Tung, he set about destroying an average of one rat a day, thus insuring food supplies were not contaminated and remained fit for human consumption. After the war Simon received a citation for "meritorious and distinguished service."

*M*y fifth life in Japan in the early Edo period was not rich in material things, but the love and kindness I received from my keeper was wealth enough. And I was able to repay that love in a most unusual way....

5

THE
BECKONING
CAT

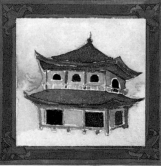

I cannot recall my arrival at Gotokuji temple; perhaps I was born there, though I have no recollection of a mother or siblings at the temple. My first memory is of the monk Tengoku.

Possibly I was an orphan. If, I had been deprived of my true mother's care, it was amply provided by Tengoku. He lavished attention on me which I did not have to share with other kittens. Moreover, he never said to me, "You're grown up. Go fend for yourself!" as most feline parents would.

As a kitten, I took all this affection for granted. It was only when I grew up and learned more of the world that I realized how lucky I was having food and fresh spring water in constant supply and being so well looked after.

Tengoku was never one to refuse an invitation to a game: often it was he who would begin one, calling, "Come along Tama!" and dangling an embroidered ball or a piece of string before me. When I was a very small kitten, it was he who carefully cleaned and groomed me. Even though I soon learned to do this for myself, he continued to remove any burrs or other twigs and foliage that got stuck to my — fortunately — short-haired coat from my expeditions in the undergrowth. He always found time each day to give my fur a thorough brushing. This not only kept my coat and short tail clear of dust and the fur on my legs and underside its natural milky-white color, but the sensation itself was most agreeable, and I always showed my thanks with loud purrs.

The shrine and the wood around it were my territory, which I claimed without any opposition. No other cat seemed to want it. In fact, in those early years I never saw another cat, though occasionally I might sniff the marks left by a stranger at the limits of my land.

There was little foliage below the pines, beyond them only bracken and a few herbs growing on a patch of stony ground. Tengoku depended upon the gifts of the faithful for his survival, and unfortunately those gifts were few. Travelers seldom stopped – we were too close to Edo for them to pause for their devotions. The local villagers could not give us much: their lives were hard, too, and they were almost as poor as we were.

I discovered that I could catch mice, rats, and even birds, but when I took them to Tengoku, he scolded me: "Tama, Tama, these are our brothers and sisters. The Buddha, in his wisdom, taught us that we must not harm them. Our duty is to help our fellow creatures."

Well, the Buddhist teaching may be true for humans, but I have not yet noticed the eagle or the owl, the snake or the fox behaving for the benefit of others. Even so, none of the creatures in the animal kingdom kill for pure pleasure, as some humans do.

I went on catching rats and mice. The holy scrolls – the folding books of prayers kept in the shrine – and the bowls of offerings had to be defended from their depredation; it was as simple as that. And if a bird should happen to fall under my claws before I could pull them back, surely no one could blame me for the accident. I made sure that Tengoku never saw me hunting, and I never again offered him my catch. It would have made me so happy to share it, but there was no point. He would only dig a little grave and chant the burial rite over the delicious morsel.

Sometimes a local farmer brought us rice or a parcel of seaweed; more rarely, there might be some fish or a small box of tea. When a traveler visited the shrine and left a coin, Tengoku could go to market and buy something for the larder, but he would always spend some of the money on incense sticks for the altar.

Tengoku shared everything he had with me. I took as little as possible without revealing that I had ways of supplementing my own diet. One year, harvests were poor and gifts even fewer than usual. By this time, the birds had learned to keep well out of my way, and I had caught all the mice for miles around.

"Eat, Tama, eat," begged Tengoku. "You are so thin that your bones are sticking out. Enjoy your supper while you can; we only have one bowl of rice left. How lucky we are that we do not have to share it with our brothers the mice."

I blushed with shame beneath my fur. He must have known about my hunting, but he did not chastise me.

I licked up a few grains and then gently tipped the bowl toward Tengoku with the tip of my nose. As I looked up into his face, I could see tears in his eyes. Never had I seen my beloved friend look so sad.

"Little cat brother, what are we going to do? Must we turn brigand and rob innocent travelers to feed our hungry bellies? Finish the bowl, and then let us meditate before Lord Buddha and pray to him for guidance."

We went into the little sanctuary and sat quietly before the figure of the Buddha. But I could not concentrate on such spiritual thoughts; my mind was wandering over other paths. Why had Tengoku mentioned brigands? I saw myself with a cloth across my face, leaping to pull a rider from his horse, wielding a sword against litter bearers and forcing some prince to hand over his jewels.

Perhaps it was then that the seed of an idea was planted. There could be no question of offering banditry and violence; there was too much of that in the world already. That was not what Tengoku had meant. Our temple at Gotokuji must always offer a welcome and a refuge. But how could that provide us with a living? We already had very little to offer by way of hospitality and were therefore becoming less likely to receive generous donations. How could I change this? I could not find the answers immediately.

Tengoku finished his devotions, and I curled up on his lap. He placed his arm around me, and suddenly I felt convinced that I would know what to do by morning.

Does guidance come in dreams? I could not be sure where the idea came from, but the next day I felt inspired. Lapping a little water and refusing any breakfast, I went out and stationed myself beside the high road. I had already missed the first travelers: a party of peasants pushing a loaded cart to market. Not another soul passed by until noon, by which time the sun was scorching. They were a band of traveling entertainers, walking along, joking and singing, but they ignored me. Next I heard hooves on the road. One of the Shogun's messengers was pounding toward me, but he galloped by without a glance. I waited there all day, with my ears sharply cocked up, my head erect, my whiskers fluffed out, and a welcoming look on my face.

It was already getting dark when the group of peasants came back from market with their empty cart. One of them recognized me and stroked my head. Through the whole day, he was the only person who seemed to see me, let alone stop and visit the shrine.

I crept back to the Temple, tired, disappointed, and starving. It was all I could do not to lap up all the rice left in the breakfast bowl which the selfless Tengoku had left untouched.

"Where have you been all day, old friend?" he said. "I thought

you'd left me to seek your fame and fortune. Come eat, you look as though you're hungry." Miserably I ate the food. My master plan had been a complete waste of time.

Next morning, all the food was gone. The concern Tengoku expressed because there was no food for me fired my resolve, and I took up my position again beside the roadway and waited patiently. No one took any notice. How could I attract attention? A farm lad I knew was passing, so I meowed and held up my paw. Why did I do it? It was an instinctive gesture I used to make as a kitten when I was hungry, and I was certainly hungry that day, so perhaps that explains it. Anyway, it did the trick. "Good morning, Tama, sorry I haven't time to stop," said the lad with a smile and a wave. My spirits lifted.

I tried raising my paw again when I heard a hunter coming down the road. He certainly saw me! Too late I smelled his dog, which he whistled to chase me. I had to take refuge up a tree trunk. It was late summer and a gloomy unsettled day, so there were depressingly few travelers on the high road.

Late in the afternoon, with the red sun already low in the sky, I heard the steady trot of several horses in the distance. As they approached, I saw it was a party of half a dozen samurai. They were not in full armor, but wore their swords as well as the bows and quivers of arrows slung over their shoulders. They carried falcons on their wrists and had been out hawking. Two of them had already

passed before a third called out to draw attention to me. They turned their horses and, as though on parade before their lord, all stood in a line opposite me.

I was a little frightened, not least of the falcons, but remained outwardly composed and elegantly positioned. I turned my head to each of them in turn, looked each of them in the eye, then raised my paw and pointed to the temple.

"This is amazing," said the eldest samurai.

"Did you ever see anything like it? How can a cat hold that position?" questioned another.

"Look the cat's pointing. It wants us to go up to the temple," said their leader.

"It must be a devil cat." This was the youngest.

"No, the cat does not have a devil's tail. It is a good cat with a short tail and anyway, no devil would direct us to visit a holy shrine."

The young samurai seemed reassured.

I lowered my paw and turned to the path, looking back over my shoulder at the astonished group.

"Let us dismount and follow. This surely is an invitation we must not refuse," declared their leader, coming down from his horse.

Tengoku heard the visitors coming up the cobbled path and came out to greet them. They told him they saw me beckoning to them and that, intrigued, they had felt bound to accept my invitation to visit the shrine.

"We are tired from our sport," they said. "We would like to rest for a while at your temple."

The monk showed the samurai where

their horses could graze beneath the trees and directed them to a shelter by the temple eaves where the falcons could be set with the jesses on their feet tied to a fence rail. I noticed now that all the birds' heads were hooded. That was why they were so quiet: they could not see. Thus bound and blinded there was no need to fear that they might swoop down to strike me with their sharp talons.

The samurai laid down their bows and took off their quivers and their sword belts before the entrance of the shrine, then slipped off their shoes before going in. In turn, they each went forward, brought their hands together to make a sharp clap, and bowed their heads to make a prayer.

When the samurai had completed their devotions, they joined Tengoku who had set out a kettle to heat and prepared the tea box and cups ready to perform the tea ceremony. After they had composed themselves, he made and offered tea in the ceremonial way using the very last of the tea that we possessed. The samurai performed each stage of the ceremony precisely and went on to join the monk in discourse. They were educated men, in service with the noble Lord Ii Naotaka of Huikone Castle. Tengoku spoke in fine words of religious duties and moral obligations. Philosophical speeches which he had so often rehearsed with me alone as audience His quiet words captivated us all, and for a while I forgot my empty belly.

While we were all listening to Tengoku, thick black clouds had filled the sky, hiding the sinking sun, and the wind had begun to blow fiercely. Its sound rose to that of a gale, and a great roll of thunder broke our tranquil mood. Outside, the horses were becoming agitated. Telling his guests to rest, Tengoku hurried out to lead their mounts to shelter beneath the temple eaves. Just then, the sky parted and torrential rain began to fall.

I had never seen such a storm; surely no cat ever has. The earth shook as great flashes of lightning streaked across the sky, glittering through the huge raindrops which fell like diamond daggers. Then hail began to fall, white and thick like hard rocks, while the rumbling explosions continued in the sky above. Everything was drenched, and it seemed as if the rushing torrents would soon rise and drown us. The horses and the falcons were deathly quiet; terrified. I cowered close to Tengoku, feeling no shame in fearing such a dreadful storm. I purred with relief as the kindly monk picked me up and held me close. The samurai sat in silence, in awe and respect of nature at her most violent.

At last the storm's fury lessened, and the thunder-rolls began to move away. The hurricane had blown itself out, and the clouds had shed all their water. As the sky cleared, a bright moon shone down on every sparkling surface. The samurai prepared to leave. The leader made a generous offering for the temple and its monk, then thanked Tengoku for his uplifting and enlightening sermon.

"It was not by chance, I'm sure," he said, "that your cat Tama welcomed us to your temple. Had it not been for the beckoning cat, we and our horses would have been exposed to the full fury of the storm with all its dangers. Who knows what might have happened. The cat brought us here and saved us. This remarkable cat has, with Buddha's blessing, given us a miraculous deliverance."

"I shall tell our Lord Ii of these events, and we will return very soon to show our thanks in greater measure."

I wanted to escort the noble samurai back to the road, but I hesitated when I saw that the stream which flowed down the path had not yet subsided. Tengoku picked me up. He slipped on his high wooden sandals and, lifting me to his shoulder, carried me down to the roadway. There I sat raising my paw in salute to the samurai as they turned in their saddles and waved back to us smiling.

The samurai did come back, bringing rich gifts and endowments for the temple. As the years passed, the Ii family showed us many favors, even choosing our shrine as the place of family burial. Though I had done so little, many people came to see "the cat who beckoned." I felt very pleased with myself, but recently I must admit I have begun to get a little tired of standing by the roadway, with my paw in the air. But people expect it, it helps us to make the temple beautiful, and it is good to see Tengoku so happy now that he is no longer hungry all the time.

However, the wise and kind Tengoku must have noticed how I have begun to feel.

"It is time for you to take it easy" he said today, adding, despite his many years. "You are no longer young. You must come in from the road, and spend the day comfortably by the shrine where you can raise a paw for those you recognize as truly devout, and not just the sightseers."

Perhaps that is what I will do tomorrow.

THE BECKONING CAT

This cat lives in Japan early in the Edo period, at the beginning of the seventeenth century. Its story is famous as that of the Maneki-neko (beckoning cat), which has become a symbol of good luck.

The Gotokuji Temple still stands in a western suburb of Tokyo, the modern name for the ancient capital of Edo.

In the past, Japan was a very stratified society. Samurai were professional warriors living by a strict code of honor, bushido. *They developed a culture, heavily influenced by Zen Buddhism, which included the tea ceremony. This is not just a matter of making, serving, and drinking tea according to a strict ritual, but also includes participation in an esthetic experience, an intellectual discourse, or the contemplation of an artistic object.*

Bobtailed cats

Cats probably first reached Japan as presents from China to the Imperial court, where they were greatly admired. Tama, the Maneki-neko, is of the indigenous bobtailed form, now known worldwide as the Japanese Bobtail breed, which has existed in Japan for many centuries. It has a short tail, rather like that of the "stumpy" form of the Manx cat, but this mutation does not appear to be associated with any harmful genetic defect. The tail is carried erect and is disguised by a pompom of fur that gives it the look of a rabbit's tail.

The tricolor, or Mi-Ke, coat, a pattern of black and red patches on white, is the most popular color for the breed, but it is recognized in most feline colors and patterns except for the agouti of the Abyssinian and the point markings of the Siamese.

Bobtailed cats feature in many Japanese paintings and woodblock prints.

The samurai

The samurai caste was rigidly separated from such lower classes as farmers, merchants, and artisans. They found a place in the service of the *daimyo*, the feudal barons of Japan, but, unlike European knights, they did not hold land. Instead, they were given an allowance by the lord to whom they owed

Japanese woodblock showing sword-wielding samurai.

allegiance. In the peaceful era which began soon after the beginning of the seventeenth century, the samurai became the stewards and chamberlains of baronial estates. Their *bushido* code of conduct placed emphasis on justice, courage, benevolence, sincerity, and loyalty, especially to their lord, and stoicism in the face of physical or mental suffering. To escape disgrace, they would commit ritual suicide, known as *hara-kiri*.

Japanese woodblock showing witch cats with split tails.

Devil cats

Witch cats and devil cats, which can take human form and include cases of vampirism, form part of Japanese folklore. They are easily identified because they have two tails, or one tail split into two. However, the split tail is not apparent at first, and kittens' tails were sometimes cut off to prevent them from turning into demons. This may have created a preference for bobtailed cats, which could not become demons development of the type at the expense of others.

Gotokuji

Tama was buried at Gotokuji which became the Beckoning Cat Temple where owners brought the ashes of their cremated cats to be interred beneath the shrine of the beckoning cat. Even today, when a cat is lost or is ill, owners write out prayers and hang them in the temple.

The temple is also famous as the burial place of Ii Naosuke, the lord whose samurai were greeted by the beckoning-cat, and for the ancient trees which grow there.

Good-luck charm

The symbol of the beckoning cat, usually reproduced in ceramic, is often displayed near shop and restaurant entrances or on counters, both to welcome people in and as a talisman for good fortune. They can be found in Japanese homes, too, to bring good luck, and at Gotokuji Temple in Tokyo, these figures are ranged in rank upon rank, the offerings of cat owners.

I began my sixth life in the early nineteenth century
as an alley cat in the markets of London town. But
destiny soon thrust me onto the surging seas, where I
had to use all my special skills to stay alive....

6

THE
THIEF'S
CAT

I didn't start life in this hot, expansive country among these strange flightless birds and animals with pockets in their bellies. I was born in the great City of London, in Spitalfields.

Life never got boring in London: every day brought with it fresh adventures. Even so, it was a hard life, and I had to be tough to survive. Tough and clever.

The city offered all kinds of possibilities: a cat could move into a house, mark out his hunting ground in an office or warehouse, even take over a church. The drawback was the long wait involved before territory fell vacant. There was certain to be a fight to claim it; you would have your work cut out for you; keeping off scavenging toms and other intruders. I found it easier to be a free-ranger.

Roaming through the streets, it was easy to find pickings in the markets – from street stands or from the displays mounted outside shops. Good timing was the trick. Choose your prize – something easy to get at and not too heavy to make off with quickly; wait 'til the seller or shopkeeper was distracted; then in and out, quick as you could. With the little morsel in my jaws – a fish, a quail, a chop – I would streak away before they even knew that it was gone.

For heavy foodstuffs, I would use one of my skillfully discovered hiding places. A cache nearby but out of sight where I could leave a chicken, a rabbit, or a piece of beef, returning to it later. Of course I ran the risk that someone else might find it and claim it. Better to hole up, eat an immediate meal, then, after dark, lug what was left to my larder for later.

It was no good working the same patch regularly. I got recognized and chased away, people watched out for "that smart-alec black and white tom." I worked my way right through the city in my time: across to Covent Garden and out as far as the Mayfair market, sometimes even across the bridge to Southwark.

One of my favorite techniques was to choose a strategic spot and settle down for a good wash, or curl up and pretend to be asleep, encouraging the passerby to stroke me. I would appear to pose no threat, but I was stationed near enough to the market stands to nip in and snatch some food when I got my chance.

One day I was following this routine just a stone's throw away from a butcher's shop. A man had stopped to stroke me, which was good cover because I was about to pounce.  Imagine my surprise when I discovered the man was up to the same game. We both went for the same smoked sausage! He got the whole string!!

I wasn't going to stand for that. It wasn't difficult to track him down. He was sitting on the steps of St. Saviour's church, eating.

"Hello," he said, "Haven't we met before?"

I indicated that I wanted my share.

"I'm Joseph," he said, "Joe to you." He cut me off a couple of sausages and offered them with an amused smile.

After sharing that first meal, we often worked together. I would attract the attention of the shopkeeper while Joe tucked something in his bag or underneath his shirt. Sometimes he'd talk to a seller while I did my dash and grab. Our partnership worked well, but we got careless. Perhaps someone had realized that we were a team and was on the lookout. Anyway Joe got nabbed. We had only stolen a loaf of bread, but however small the booty, stealing was considered a heinous crime. He was hauled off by officers of the law.

When Joe didn't show up for a day or two, I thought I'd better find out what had happened to him. They had thrown him into jail. I found him in a cell in Newgate. He was on short rations — mainly gruel and water — so I kept an eye out for small things I could snitch and smuggle down to him. It is easy for us cats to stroll in and out of prison buildings bold as brass, though not if you're carrying anything. I had to slip through bars and slink around shadowy corners if I was taking him a chicken leg or a morsel of pie.

There wasn't much Joe could do. He'd been caught red-handed. The judge didn't care that he stole because he was hungry and there were no jobs for him to earn a penny so he could pay for food. They sentenced him to "transportation." I didn't really understand what it meant. I picked a bit up from Joe's talk with other prisoners, and he tried to explain it to me: "I'm leavin' the country, going on a long journey. In short, it's goodbye, me old chum."

Life was much tougher operating on my own again. It wasn't just that Joe and I had helped each other with the hunting. In the past, no matter where and when Joe dossed down, I would curl up with him for warmth and safety. I never had to worry about being cold when Joe was around. We had been a good team, and I decided if Joe was taking off, I was going with him.

That evening I went to see Joe in his cell and spend the night. It was as well that I chose that day to visit, because if I hadn't gone then I would have been left behind. The next morning, Joe was chained to two other prisoners, marched up to the prison yard, and shoved into a wagon. I ran behind the wagon and caught up with it near London Bridge. I managed to jump onto a cross piece just below the main body of the wagon and out of sight. The jolting of the cobbles put all my bones ajangle.

The wagon finally stopped at a dock on the other side of the Thames; the men were herded up a wooden walkway onto a ship.

I hung around waiting for an opportunity to get aboard the *Majestic,* but the gangplank was clearly in view of the ship's crew. After three days, a flurry of activity indicated the *Majestic* was soon to sail. It was now or never. I didn't use the gangplank, but chose a thick hauser running from the dock to the bulwarks. Suddenly I was aboard.

The *Majestic* was like a city in itself. It took several days to explore. Joe and the other prisoners were chained in berths below, and there were soldiers and sailors patrolling the ship, even at night. I was worried that there didn't seem to be much food around. In the almost empty holds, there was a promising smell of rats – but I was out of practice at catching my own. After a couple of days, I found the galley. That was more like it, packed with all sorts of delicious edibles, but I knew it would be difficult to raid. That was where I got caught.

The chef who caught me had a cleaver in his hand. I cowered in a corner. Then his face broke into a smile.

"Well, well, my lovely, and I thought you was a big rat! Have more, we c'n spare a bite from Cap'n's chop."

Could I trust him? Would he put me in irons like they had done with Joe? I decided to eat the chop. I had a terrible hunger on me.

"Well cat, what's yer name?" Cook asked as he stroked me. "I think I'll call you Drake. This ship be needin' a cat."

It seemed as if I'd fallen on my feet. We docked the following

day, and I was in a quandary over whether to stay on board or not. Then I saw sacks of food, sides of beef, ducks and cattle being loaded aboard. That decided it for me – I would stay. There would be food enough for months. More people boarded as well, not in chains, but carrying boxes and bundles full of possessions.

When we set sail again, the weather was not too good. At least I didn't have to hide now. As the wind got stronger, the sea rocked the ship from side to side in a violent, rolling motion. Some of the passengers and the poor prisoners down below held their bellies and retched, but I never felt sick. Once we were on the high seas, the prisoners were freed of their chains. In fair weather they were allowed to exercise on the rear deck. I went over to say hello to Joe, but I had put on a lot of weight and was not sure he recognized me.

One day, when I asked for my dinner, Cook shouted "No! It's time you started working for your living, Drake…" With that, he picked me up and took me down to the stores.

"Rats!" he said, pointing to where they had been gnawing at a sack of ship's biscuits. Then he left me.

Oh, dear, I was expected to work for my keep. Well, there was no way I could turn back! I tried out a few of my old rat-catching techniques on some rope ends in a corner. I certainly was out of practice, but gradually the old skills came back to me. Suddenly I realized several pairs of eyes were watching and – woosh! – I got one of them and rushed off with it to the galley.

After some weeks, we stopped to take on water and fresh stores, but we didn't dock. We anchored offshore, and small boats brought everything out to us. Then we sailed on, the weather becoming hotter and hotter. I had previously thought there was nothing nicer than spending the long days lazing in the sun, but now I began to look for shade. We sailed for weeks without sight of land; then we passed the equator, and the days gradually started getting cooler once more.

I had made many friends on board in addition to Cook – and I had identified some enemies, too. Some of the soldiers thought it a fine joke to pull my tail; worse still, a sailor trapped me under a swabbing bucket. I was furious: I scratched his face when I got out and he threatened to throw me overboard. Only rarely would I venture down to the convicts' deck. It stank. Once I carried a titbit down to Joe, but it caused a fight among the prisoners, and some of them tried to corner me. Our partnership was over. Even when he came on deck, I felt I must keep my distance. I couldn't afford to put myself or Joe at risk of violence from the others.

One morning, the convicts and the whole ship's company were made to parade on deck. I watched with interest as Joe was marched up a gangway. Then, to my horror, his shirt was torn from his back, and he was stretched out in the shape of a cross with his wrists and ankles tied down to a grating. Hardly a sound broke his lips as a marine gave him twenty lashes. I could see the hard leather cutting into his back. The whip they used was called a cat-o-nine-tails, and I thought it was ironic that this brutal weapon should be linked by its name to my species. I never did discover what he had been punished for, but the experience of witnessing such savagery terrified me. I decided I must leave the ship whenever I got the chance.

Before we saw land again, we passed through a belt of foul weather. Huge waves broke over the ship. Everything not firmly tied down slid from one side of the vessel to the other. I went below but a wave crashed through a hatchway and nearly drowned me. I found refuge in the cabin belonging to Emma, a lady passenger who had taken it upon herself to give me a daily grooming.

While she clung to her bed, I dug my claws into the floorboards of the cabin to stop myself from being thrown against the walls. Soon I discovered I could match the movement of the rolling ship, so I jumped up to join Emma, and we wedged ourselves in her bunk to keep from us falling out and cushioned ourselves with blankets.

The next revictualling stop was below a mountain which soared to the sky, but was chopped off at the top like a table. Again, small boats plied to and fro, but I was shipbound, with no chance of escape. There had been no more flogging incidents, and my fears had subsided a little, but being a sea-cat was becoming boring.

It got worse; the next part of the voyage seemed to go on forever. There was Emma, the cook, and my other friends, but I felt the need for new faces and fresh fields. To amuse myself, I began to go below deck to chase rats without cook's instigation. My skill improved greatly with practice. I was so fast that eventually it got to the stage that I had to deliberately let some escape or there would have been no rodents left alive to keep me active.

There were a few other excitements during our long voyage on the *Majestic*. One day a huge fish, almost as big as our ship, swam alongside, half out of the waves, spouting water from its head. All the crew members rushed to the side of the boat shouting "Look at the whale!" when suddenly it dived, lashing the water with its huge tail, drenching all those watching, including me.

After several months at sea, the thrill of sailing had gone. Now I found the high sea and its savage storms frightening rather than exciting. I simply longed to get my paws on dry land again.

Eventually, after weeks of anticipation, I heard the call, "Land Ahoy," and we got our first glimpse of land on the horizon. We had to sail along the coast for days and days before we found a cove to tuck into, but nobody minded, we were all greatly cheered by the prospect of finally reaching our destination.

Emma was busy repacking her boxes. The moment of truth had arrived; I had to decide which of my friends to stick with. The cook showed no sign of packing his belongings, so I guessed that he would be staying with the ship. That I could not do. Joe was in chains again. I couldn't see a future with him; when I saw how small the town was, I guessed its markets would not offer us much opportunity for a partnership. Emma, however, was making a great fuss of me.

"Oh, Drake, Emma's going to miss her lovely, velvety tomcat," she simpered, almost smothering me with her caresses. She seemed the best bet – but could I put up with this kind of attention?

Before we docked, a boat rowed out, and a stylish man came aboard and greeted Emma. She flung her arms around him, introduced me, then immediately gave me a tear-stained farewell! I had to think quickly. The man looked important. His house must have a well-stocked larder. Emma's bags and boxes were loaded into the boat, and she was helped down a rope ladder. I jumped after.

I curled up on Emma's lap, and no one objected. The *Majestic* would have to find itself a kitten from another ship in the little fleet to do its rat-catching. Once ashore, Emma got her husband and myself into a carriage, and we drove to the outskirts of the town. A short time later, we arrived at a magnificent mansion with a long, sweeping driveway. As I stepped up onto the elegant veranda, I realized that I had made the right decision. First they showed me through to the kitchen, offering me some juicy chicken and a bowl of water. Then after a quick wash and a nap, I set out exploring.

Hunting was easy, most of the animals seemed never to have seen a cat before. Even so, I was definitely not expected to stock my own larder. In fact, Emma disapproved if she caught me with prey. I had enjoyed a great deal of sport in catching the ship's rats, and I wasn't going to give up hunting, so it became my secret game. I could still do a useful job in keeping vermin down, but I knew it would be better not to let the sensitive Emma know of it.

I sometimes miss the hurly-burly of London's streets and wonder what became of poor Joe, who was taken off to a camp for long years of hard labor. But I have no regrets about coming to Australia. I have a good life here with plenty to eat, friends to hunt with, and lots of space for adventures…and the sunshine here certainly beats the rain and smog of London!

THE THIEF'S CAT

This cat begins its life in early nineteenth-century London before setting out on the long and arduous journey to the other side of the world on a convict ship.

A sentence of transportation was relatively common at this time. It helped to reduce pressure on overcrowded prisons and provided workers for the development of colonial settlements overseas.

Instead of hugging the west coast of Africa, ships sailing to the Indian Ocean often followed the much longer route across the Atlantic to South America and back again, because this took advantage of prevailing winds and ocean currents.

Some convict ships carried livestock for the colony, although animals may also have been killed on the voyage to provide fresh meat. Most meat would have been salted or otherwise preserved to last the many weeks of the voyage.

Scene from the
Robber Kitten
dated 1858.

Lasting relationship

Cats are strongly territorial animals, even as domestic pets, but many show an identification with a human who has been an important part of their life which is stronger than their links with a particular place. There are many reports of cats that have sought out such humans, sometimes over very long distances (see page 113). One famous instance was a cat belonging to the Earl of Southampton (above), patron of William Shakespeare. The Earl was imprisoned in the Tower of London because of his involvement in a rebellion against Queen Elizabeth I.

Here his cat sought him out. It was most likely a cat living at the Earl's London house, not one from his country mansion many miles away, but nevertheless, how did it know where to look? And how did it find a way through the guards and fortifications and down the chimney of the very room in which his master was imprisoned? The surviving record of this happening was written many years later, but a painting by John de Critz the Elder, painted at the time, shows him with a personable black and white cat, with a view of the Tower of London inserted in the top right corner of the picture.

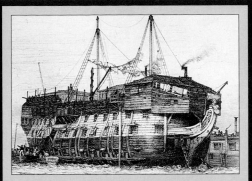

Convict ships

Transportation was first used by both England and Portugal as a means of providing labor for their colonies. When the American War of Independence prevented convicts from being sent to America which found a plentiful supply of black slaves instead, England used transportation as a way of establishing a colony in Australia.

While waiting for transportation, many convicts spent months in prison "hulks" like the one above converted from unseaworthy vessels. The first convict ships sailed for Australia in May, 1787, reaching Botany Bay in modern New South Wales in January, 1788. Transportation continued until 1868 when the last convict ships arrived in Western Australia. Modern Australia dates its existence as a state from the arrival of the "First Fleet" of convict ships in 1788.

Transportation not only provided a workforce where it was needed, but avoided the problem of having to provide jails. It was used to punish crimes not serious enough for the death penalty, but for which it was thought flogging was too lenient. Sometimes death penalties were commuted to transportation. When penal reform ended hanging as a penalty for theft and other such crimes, the numbers available for transportation greatly increased.

Tolpuddle martyrs

After serving part of their sentence, convicts were commonly released on "ticket of leave," a form of parole, to work outside the prison settlements. When their complete sentence was up, they could return to Britain. The cost of doing so, and the opportunities the new land offered compared with what they had left behind, meant that most stayed, although some of the famous group of farm-workers from Tolpuddle in Dorset, who were sentenced to transportation for founding the world's first trade union, did eventually return.

A demonstration petitioning for the remission of the sentence on the Tolpuddle Martyrs in 1834.

Working passage

The inventory of supplies for the "First Fleet" in 1787 included kittens, and cats usually formed part of any ship's complement to keep vermin in check, but ship's cats were not just working animals. Francesco Moresina, a seventeenth-century Venetian admiral, is said never to have sailed without his pet cat, and in 1553 an English sailor on a Venetian ship recorded how when the cat fell overboard, a boat was lowered and went back half a mile to rescue her. Japanese sailors used to consider a tortoiseshell cat aboard particularly lucky. They believed cats could foretell approaching storms (perhaps by their reactions to changing barometric pressure) and that if they were sent up to the top of the mast could frighten storm demons away.

Extinction

The introduction of new species can unbalance local ecology. In Australia and New Zealand, imported cats and other predators had a disastrous effect on some native species, especially flightless birds. Some endemic small island species were completely exterminated. On the Frigate Island in the Seychelles, for instance, feral cats introduced by other countries are believed to have been responsible for the virtual extinction of the Seychelles Magpie-robin. The Galápagos Hawk is similarly endangered.

*A*t last, after the excitement and upheaval of my previous few lives, my seventh is spent as a demi-monde in Paris toward the end of the nineteenth century. Such luxury! These artistic types think they know it all, but I can teach them a thing or two....

7

THE
ARTIST'S
CAT

One was always being admired. "Thank you, my dear, that's very kind of you. But one's appearance after all is something one inherits. Of course, one must take care of one's looks. Overindulgence of any kind must be avoided. Take cream only in moderation and always, *always*, insist on perfect grooming, especially when you have such a luxurious Persian coat as mine. I persist in completing the finishing touches myself."

Being blessed with shapely form, fine fur, and perfect features imposes great responsibilities. It is not vanity but duty to look one's best. Of course, I have received many immoderate compliments on my beauty, but they count for nothing. Even as a kitten my appearance set heads turning, but do not think that my exquisite looks made life easy. Not every tom's a gentleman, as I'm sure any feline would tell you. They were especially uncouth where I grew up, in the raucous, rowdy atmosphere of the Moulin Rouge. Naturally, I expected to go into show business, but I could never see myself high-kicking and frou-frouing skirts with the chorus line. No, no. The can-can was definitely not my style. Though the Moulin Rouge was where I made my debut at a very early age.

Quite without consultation, I was made to partner that famous English *chanteuse* Miss May Belfort when she sang her celebrated song "I've Got a Pussy Cat." Of course, it's not me in Compte Henri de Toulouse-Lautrec's poster of her. That scrawny black thing was her usual partner, who looked suspiciously like the poor creature in that scandalous painting, Monsieur Edouard Manet's *Olympia*. I was pushed on to replace her when she suddenly decided to produce a litter of kittens. For me the song made no sense. That stupid lament: "Daddy wouldn't buy me a bow-wow" – why should anyone want a dog with me around! – but my first performance did attract a great deal of admiration.

However, the career I had mapped out for myself in those days was on a much higher artistic level. I had the makings of a great ballet dancer. Daily I would practice my *plié* and *pas de chat*, showing very great promise as a prima ballerina. But it was not to be.

One day, I was concentrating so hard on practicing my *entrechats*, I failed to notice a band of urchins approach with a dog. They shouted "After it!" to the canine beast, sending the horrid animal to chase me. It was a big, fast-running hound that could easily have outstripped me over a distance. I took evasive action, and after a short chase leapt onto a wall and then up on the roof. I couldn't resist spitting at the impotent dog down below. That was my mistake. I was so busy putting the barking lout in his place that I did not see one of the boys pull out a slingshot. A sharp stone struck me, cutting into my left rear leg. I nearly lost my footing. If it had been a front paw, I would have fallen straight into those waiting teeth; luckily, I managed to cling on until a passing gentleman saw my plight and chased the rogues away.

The leg healed, of course, but not with the same strength. My dedicated training had been in vain. My pirouetting days were over. I would have to make my mark on the world in some other way; I was *not* going to end up producing countless kittens and watching boring mouse holes. Perhaps I could be a ballet-maker. My head was full of ideas for dances, but where was the opportunity to use them? Where were the feline ballet troupes to offer me employment for my choreographic skills? I might have become an actress in the legitimate theater, but the roles available were few, and if you will forgive me for being so coarse, to be an "actress" in those days was not an entirely respectable occupation.

Apart from my forced appearances at the Cabaret, I had not been much seen in public. I realized I had to make myself known; I had to procure contacts in the world of society, art, and letters to promote my new career. It actually proved to be very easy.

By that time I had blossomed into a gorgeous young cat, and I was, of course, impeccably groomed. These assets, plus the further advantage of the elegance provided by my ballet training, were a winning combination. Still it was truly a surprise that I, Minette, attracted so much attention just by walking through a room. I had only to make a momentary appearance for the compliments to flow.

"Oh, regard her luxurious, long tail."

"Look at that perfect pink nose."

"Those dainty white paws, *c'est jolie*."

The artist gentlemen present reached for their sketchpads and pencils. My new vocation beckoned.

However, I never liked such phrases as "artist's model." The Montmartre dancing girls, along with others who knew no better, might strike indecent poses for painters and do who knows what else besides. But I preferred to think of myself as a feline society lady who allowed her portrait to be painted; *I* always posed with the maximum of grace and decorum. Not that I would breathe a word against those aforementioned lovely young women. They always treated me with kindness and respect, and often brought me special offerings of tasty morsels. Indeed, it was one of them who took me to pose in a double portrait with her in the studio of Monsieur... let us say Monsieur X, for I would not wish to draw attention to his association with that particular young woman. Although for a time I took up residence there, I soon moved on to a much better address.

I found myself a welcome visitor in the *ateliers* of the celebrated artists who lived in the most fashionable parts of Paris. During these studio visits, I must have met every significant figure in contemporary cultural circles. Of course I modeled for M. Steinlen, dancing for him as he quickly sketched. Certainly I taught young Colette Willy a thing or two, which she later put to good effect. The critic Theodore Duret made a great fuss of me, which made me wonder why no invitation came to visit Lulu, the cat who presided in his house. Pierre Renoir often sketched me, preferring me as a model even when he had to modify my shape and add tabby pattern or blotching from scribbled notes he had made of a commissioned subject who could not hold a pose. I was flattered, and not just by his appreciation of my professional skill. On one visit, he admitted to me that on occasions he was forced not to paint my furry beauty in its full glory for fear of eclipsing the somewhat voluptuous charms of the human ladies who made up the composition.

Now who else was there? So many people painted portraits of

me that I really can't recall all of them. Many of the paintings cannot be found in galleries open to the *hoi polloi*, as they were purchased immediately for private collections. They seldom come on the market. They are works which no one with a true appreciation of art and beauty would ever part with.

The Impressionists, of course, all painted me. They could not resist the play of light on my superb fur. "Minette," they would say, "your fur is gorgeous, almost incandescent!"

They painted me right up until I was an old cat. But to see me at my best, you have to see paintings of me when I was young.

It was not only as an artist's model that I made my great contribution to French art, though my exciting discovery has never been credited to me. M. Seurat and M. Signac both owe me a great debt. It was I who invented *pointillism*.

Just before I made this breakthrough, I had been feeling very frustrated, surrounded by so many creative people, yet unable to unleash my own artistic flair. I had taken the opportunity to observe and study many artists at their easels, and

I had gained a deep understanding of their craft. I decided it was time that I, too, became a painter. At night, I crept into the studio and tried to paint with the brushes held between my teeth. My problem was controlling the movement and the pressure of the brush strokes. Furthermore, I could not devise a way to mix two colors together to create a new one: to mix green from yellow and blue, say.

Then one day I saw the obvious. While my painter friend had gone to the café for an absinthe, leaving paints still freshly mixed on his palette, I boldly took one paw to the cobalt blue and walked across the canvas, then went back and took a dab of the cadmium yellow on the other paw. The effect was best when I let all four paws carry different colors at once, building up a vibrant web of color and texture.

I had nearly completed this masterpiece when my current host came back from the café with a group of friends, M. Seurat among them. I saw the expression on his face when he noticed what I'd done, though when I caught his eye, he quickly looked away.

One dilemma held up the demonstration of my talent. I had to find a satisfactory way of cleaning the unwanted color from my paws. Turpentine damaged my pawpads if they were dipped into it and licking the paint off was out of the question: most of it tasted awful, and some was dangerously poisonous.

It was going to take a lot of thought to find a solution. I was just setting my mind to the task when I was invited to visit M. Seurat's studio. What did I see? He had stolen my technique!

On the easel was a canvas made up of multicolored pawprints imitated with a brush. His work drew a lot of attention, although, I must admit, not much approval. I am confident my original work would have met with much acclaim, but my innovation had been stolen. Any work of mine would now risk being labeled derivative, and I could not live with that accusation. Nor had I any way in which I could prove such a calumny to be unfounded – my own work had been painted over, and of the gentlemen who arrived with M. Seurat, only he had noticed the distinctive technique of my "work in progress."

I abandoned my painterly aspirations without ever gaining renown for my work. It was perhaps some comfort to know how little success M. Seurat had; my superior talent would not have been so easily extinguished had he not betrayed me. Worse than this theft, in the famous painting where my distinctive influence is obvious – that awkward study of the river bank on Sunday – he gave great prominence to awful canine creatures. I have never forgiven him the insult. I suppose the picture sums him up – a "Sunday painter."

However, it is not in my nature to draw attention to the failings of the other creatures, and all of these events occurred long ago. Besides, it is not public acclaim that matters, but one's own inner satisfaction. Instead of pursuing such secondary talents as I had with paint and canvas, I have concentrated on my primary artistic skills. And thanks to my ballet training I have been able to make the most of my natural elegant line and graceful movement; arts I have passed on to my children. And, I must admit, in recent years I have taken some pleasure in the successes my grandchildren have had in these new competitive gatherings of feline beauty, both here in Paris and in England where they started. Of course, they inherit their sparkling fur and kohl-marked eyes from me. But, for myself, I am content to have been immortalised by so many of my more famous contemporaries. Most of all, I am happy to look back on a life so full of beauty and intellectual stimulation. I hope that you, my dears, will one day be able to say the same.

THE ARTIST'S CAT

Minette is a beautiful Chinchilla Persian who lives in late nineteenth-century Paris.

The Bal du Moulin Rouge, opened in 1889 in Montmartre, a northern suburb of Paris, was a luxurious establishment where clientele could dance as well as watch lively entertainment. As early as 1830, some millers and bakers in Montmartre turned their establishment on the top of the hill into a dance hall, the Moulin de la Gallete. As the century progressed, Montmartre became an area with many places of entertainment where the respectable lower middle classes went to dance on a Sunday afternoon, though at night the area's low-life brought an element of risk.

G. C. A., Paris   794 Montmartre. — La rue Pigalle — Nouvelle Athènes.

Domestication

Long-haired cats began to appear in western Europe in the sixteenth century. They were probably Angora cats from Turkey. Later, a heavier and even longer-coated type arrived from Persia (modern Iran). The two types were allowed to mate indiscriminately, and by the time cat shows began in the nineteenth century, the Persian predominated. The Persian breed, as it is known in the United States though now officially called the Longhair on the British show bench, has a more flattened face than the shorthairs and the Angora, and has beautiful big eyes.

The Chinchilla is one of the most stunning of the long-haired beauties. The sparkling appearance of its fur is created by a black tip to the end of each hair. There is also a black rim to the skin around the eyes and black outlining the cat's pink nose which adds emphasis to these features.

Les Decadents

May Belfort was an Irish girl in London who made a speciality of old folk songs and spirituals. In Paris, where she appeared at several establishments, she met the famous painter Henri de Toulouse-Lautrec at a cabaret called Les Decadents in 1895. For several weeks, he took her under his wing, making oil paintings and several lithographs of her. For her performance she dressed like a very little girl and appeared with a black cat in her arms to sing (in English) in rather bleating tones:

"Daddy wouldn't buy me a bow-wow,
I've got a little cat, I'm very fond of that,
But I want a little bow-wow-wow...."

For some months Lautrec sang this brief refrain in heavily accented English as he worked, and he made a New Year card and decorated a menu for May with the little black cat. Although he soon lost interest in her, his poster of her has guaranteed that her name will be remembered.

Pointillism

George Seurat's technique of *pointillisme*, painting little dots of different colors close together so that the eye mixes the colors to form different shades and hues – rather than mixing color on the palette – can produce a vibrant effect. Seurat had previously worked in a technique much like that of the other impressionists. Paul Signac worked in a way similar to Seurat, though with rather larger brush strokes, and Camille Pissarro also tried the technique. Their colleagues thought that their work ought to be exhibited in a separate room. When the paintings were unveiled, one critic joked: "The City has ordered the exhibition to be closed because three visitors have succumbed to smallpox caused by standing in front of a painting composed entirely of dots."

Cat woman

Colette, famous as a writer of stories such as *Gigi* and *Cheri,* was a performer in her younger days and among other roles appeared in the character of a cat. She always had a cat of her own.

In the picture

Cats appear in the work of many artists. Up to the Renaissance, they are usually used symbolically. Sometimes they are used to represent fecundity, and sometimes they appear as a symbol of evil powers. Even when shown as an apparent playful pet in a Nativity scene, they may also be intended as a reminder of the forces against which the baby Jesus will have to do battle. Later, with the development of genre painting, which aimed to record domestic and other scenes more naturally, cats were often shown as pets and farmyard animals. Veronese, Dürer, Goya, Rembrandt, Hogarth, and other masters through to Picasso have included powerful cat images in their work, but few painters have specialized in cats.

During the nineteenth century, Gottfried Mind, a painter besotted with cats, gained an international reputation for his feline works, as did Henrietta Ronner-Knip, while in Japan painters such as Kuniyoshi often featured cats in their woodblock prints. Although he made one painting of a boy with a cat, most of Pierre August Renoir's cats appear in portraits of women, like the one shown (right). In the early twentieth century, Louis Wain's anthropomorphic images of cats engaged in human activities became very popular and are often reproduced as postcards, while Fujita, a later Japanese artist working in Paris, is especially remembered for his endearing cat portraits.

The Cat and Kitten *by Fujita (1886-1968).*

Girl with Cat *by Renoir (1841-1919).*

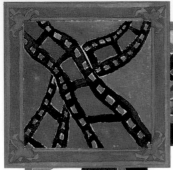

Lassie, Rin Tin Tin, and Trigger have nothing on me
— in my eighth life on Broadway in the 1930s, I was a
MEGASTAR! But it wasn't easy getting to the top...
like all the best movie stars, my climb was
fraught with adventure....

8

THE
MOVIE
CAT

I was born into show business in a wardrobe trunk inside the Prince's Theater on 42nd Street. There was never any doubt that I would be a theater cat like my mother. But what kind of theater cat? "There lies the rub," as the Bard put it.

Almost before my eyes were open, I had learned to make a good entrance — and never to come on through the fireplace! I soon mastered spitting at the villain, and how to die with grace, breathing carefully so no one could tell that I was still alive. My family had been in the business for generations, so I had an instinct for these things.

In addition to what Mother taught me of show business traditions and performing skills, I had the advantage of a kittenhood spent watching some of the best performers in the trade. From them I picked up all kinds of tricks. I was soon playing my first role as the heroine's confidante in *A Time for Remembering*. Later when Mother was indisposed after eating some shrimp that were none too fresh, I stepped into the breach and took over her role in the witch scenes of *Macbeth*.

Like all stage-struck youngsters, in my dreams I saw my name in lights above the marquee on Broadway. However, I was fully prepared to serve my apprenticeship, honing my skills in supporting roles. But I had hardly begun when I was kitnapped by a bunch of hoodlums.

Even before they let me out of the bag, the smell of glue and greasepaint told me I was in a theater. It was the Vaudeville in

Brooklyn. My spirits rose; this was a darned unorthodox way of offering me an engagement, but if I had to work in the sticks to gain experience....At least any mistakes I made would not be exposed to those butchers, the Broadway critics.

I was given a bowl of milk and shown a basket in the prop room which was to be my lodgings. Then I had a cat nap so as to be fresh when I was called for rehearsal. But I wasn't called. There wasn't even a walk-on role. Soon I discovered that I was expected to do the chores of a prop room cat and no more: chasing mice under the stage, keeping an eye on who came in and out at the artists' entrance when the stage-doorman had been at the bottle. I was never allowed even a whisker in the limelight! I decided the Vaudeville was no place for me. I had to get away.

My kittenhood had been very sheltered. I don't remember once leaving the Prince's Theater; the farthest I had gotten was sunbathing on the fire escape. The plays performed there had taught me something about the outside world, but I had no real first-hand experience of it. I didn't even know how to find my way out of Brooklyn and back to Broadway. I needed friends and quickly. Fortunately, Brooklyn proved to be the place to find them.

One night I screwed up my courage and abandoned the stage-door to check out the neighborhood. I soon found the local cats' meeting place and invited all the locals to come and see the show at the Vaudeville to get them on my side. It went down well. At the next performance, I pushed an exit door ajar and my guests slipped in, sitting themselves comfortably in the stage-left box. Shortly after this visit, my friends devised a plan for me. Through a chain of contacts, I was promised help to get as far as Manhattan. A couple of weeks later, I set out. Another adventure was about to begin, and although I felt very nervous, it was also tremendously exciting.

My journey was plain sailing until I reached the East River and had to cross Brooklyn Bridge. I decided to wait until the early hours of the morning when the traffic would not be so heavy. I was going to cross at road level – no point in climbing all the way up to the public walkway. To avoid the taxicabs and trucks, I leaped up onto the balustrade. But jumpin' Jehosphat! I hadn't reckoned on the wind. I nearly got blown straight over. It's all a matter of balance, and you can't dig your claws into a metal rail.

Manhattan was sparkling with lights, but I couldn't allow myself to enjoy the spectacle yet. I had to concentrate on my stability. Not allowing the view to distract me, I reached the other side of the bridge and was able to look down on the ships docked along the quays stretching out from the waterfront. Walking straight on brought me to City Hall where I rested in the park. A local cat gave me directions, – Broadway was close by.

When, at last, I reached 42nd Street, the Prince's Theater was "dark," not even a future play advertised. I didn't dare go through the stage-door – it was the door-keeper who had helped the kitnappers put me in the sack. I tried the fire escape and found an open window, but there was no sign of any member of my family. Had they *all* been as rudely removed as I had been? Perhaps they had gone off on tour or were spending a month or two in summer stock.

In those days it was easy to recognize an actor or an actress: they dressed with more exuberance than most, and there was always that slight hint of greasepaint in their scent. I soon discovered the cafés and bars where they met, and I eavesdropped on conversations, hoping to hear of plays being cast and auditions I could attend. Nothing, but nothing, seemed to be happening. Perhaps if I got an agent? I tried them all. The result was always the same:

"Get that god-awful cat out of here!"

I was picking myself up from the rain-swept sidewalk, having been booted downstairs yet again, when a friendly, happy-go-lucky voice asked: "Hey, junior, you all right?"

You have to be careful with strangers around Times Square, but this old tom seemed harmless enough.

"I'm Frankie. Come to my place. You'll be warm and dry, and I'll find you a bite to eat. My joint's only around the corner".

The place Frankie led me to seemed very familiar. We edged our way around a partly-open door and through some heavy curtains. Yes, we were in an auditorium. There were voices and music, but instead of actors on the stage there were two huge faces. Frankie was a moving-picture-theater cat. He showed me to his private quarters, and while I dried off my coat, he brought me a sardine from his larder.

By the time I had polished it off and was licking my whiskers, I had almost forgotten that boot up my backside. In show business you have to be resilient. Nevertheless, Frankie served sympathy with his sardines, and soon I had spilled out all my troubles.

"Right," Frankie decided, "What you need is a little diversion. The intermission has just finished. Let's go and see the show." He led me to the top step of the center aisle, where we got a splendid view without one head in the way. "Keep well to the side," he said, "We don't want the ice-cream girl stepping on your tail!"

There was a trailer for a cowboy picture, with lots of horses, then the main feature started. The hero was a bit of a wimp, I thought, and the bad guy overacted, but the lovely heroine was a natural cryer with great big tears rolling down her soft cheeks. The audience loved her. Even better from my perspective was her companion, a lovely silver tabby cat who purred to perfection, providing a most delicate understatement as she licked the heroine's tears away. That image drove out all my other memories of the movie.

"You enjoy that, Rick?" Frankie asked when we were back in his cozy corner. "Nothing wrong with a bit of sentiment. She was lovely, wasn't she? Now, that's what you should do. Don't waste time looking for non-existent parts in Broadway. Go west, young man!

"If I was younger perhaps I would come with you, but I'm a New Yorker through and through. I've a comfortable enough life here and – well – having a good top step in my own cinema makes me very popular with the lady cats.... But you – you ought to be in movies. And this is just the time. These new talkies are all the rage, and they need actors with a theater background. Now, this is what you do...."

Frankie had my future all planned. I don't think I was the first young hopeful to whom he'd given this advice. No wagon train for me. I was going to travel in comfort on the railroad. First I had to get to Chicago, then change railroads to travel on to Los Angeles. There I would find Hollywood, center of the motion picture industry.

Fortunately, Frankie was a cat who had connections; these, he said, would smooth the way. At Grand Central Station he introduced me to the conductor's cat on the night train to Chicago. I was smuggled into a comfortable berth in the luggage compartment and, when things were quiet, was invited down to share a meal in the kitchen of the restaurant car. When we reached Chicago, a resident station cat showed me where I could get a meal and pointed out a good place to nap. The next day, the same tom picked me up and took me to the tracks of the Santa Fe Railroad to embark on the second stage of the journey.

The Santa Fe's cat was very proud of his train, which was equipped for its long-haul journey with restaurant cars, sleeping compartments, and observation coaches. When most of the passengers were in their bunks, he took me on a tour along the train's vast length. In the empty observation coach we could jump up on the seats and look out of the windows; the heartland of America stretched out before us in the moonlight.

For two days we rushed on, across Utah and up into the Rockies. At last we reached Los Angeles. I carefully groomed my host to show appreciation for his kindness. We said our goodbyes, but not before he had pointed out the place beneath a bench in the ticket hall to make contact with other railroad cats if I wanted to go traveling again.

Now I was on my own. I was quivering with excitement. This was it. Mr. De Mille, here I come! But it wasn't like New York, with its busy streets, bars, sidewalk cafés, and street cats everywhere ready to point you on the way. Now I couldn't find the agents' offices or the audition rooms. Where were Metro-Goldwyn-Mayer, Paramount, Universal, and the other fantasy factories?

Then I had a stroke of luck. I'd gone back to the railroad terminal – it was a fixed point for orientation, and there was a fifty-fifty chance of pastrami at the luncheon counter. I thought I might meet a traveler going back East who could put me right on this Los Angeles scene. What I discovered was even better. There, at the end of the tracks, were huge arc lamps, a chair labeled DIRECTOR, and what I guessed must be a movie camera. Now was the chance to introduce myself. Perhaps it wasn't Mr. De Mille, but I didn't care, as long as he gave me the break I needed to launch my new career.

He threw me off his lap. "Get rid of this god-awful cat!"

I'd been looking my most charming and purring gently. Was this going to be the Times Square boot all over again?

There was a lot of shouting, then everyone got quiet, and a train came down the track with people leaning from the windows. Then someone shouted "Cut!" An actress was filmed getting off the train a dozen times or more. This was all a revelation to me. As a theater actor, I'd always had to get it right first time!

"That's it, folks!" yelled the director. "Miss Eagles, wardrobe would be grateful if you'd call in for a fitting back at the studio."

My ears pricked up when I heard "studio." I followed Miss Eagles to a white limosine without anyone noticing me. As the uniformed chauffeur came around to open the door for her, I jumped into the back. As we drove off, I saw a pair of eyes looking at me: it was the peak-capped chauffeur looking in the driver's mirror. He winked and didn't say a thing!

Our chauffeur sounded his horn, and the gates in front of us were swung open as we turned into Paramount Studios. He took Miss Eagles to the wardrobe block, but signaled to me to stay right where I was, then drove on to the commissary, went in, and brought out lunch!

"Say thanks to your new pal Carlo," he said. I was purring without any prompting. Hollywood was looking good – it got better.

"Say, fella, you got your paws and whiskers clean?" Carlo asked as I finished my ablutions after eating. "I gotta go pick up some dumb actor, but first I got you a nice surprise."

We drove around the corner, past some Egyptian pyramids,

along a street of New York brownstones and into a medieval square. He lifted me down and put me in the center by an old stone fountain. "You just wait there," he said. "I'll be seein' ya!" Then he gently whistled: two notes, one high one low, and quietly drove away.

I waited. Nothing happened. I walked around the fountain. Then I heard the sweetest meow imaginable. My ears focused, then my eyes. There, at the top of the church steps, was the Silver Tabby from the motion picture I saw in Frankie's movie theater. Slowly I walked toward her and rubbed my nose against her silvery cheek.

If it had been a movie, that would have been where the music welled up, a sunset filled the screen, and the curtains slowly closed. For us it was only the beginning. Sylvie and I have been inseparable ever since. Hollywood has been our home – we can move in any place we like when we need a vacation or a change of scene: a German castle, a Spanish palace, an English cottage, or a beach hut in Tahiti. We can play out our love scenes anywhere in the world, provided the location is on the studio backlot! I hardly ever leave the studio, unless Carlo has to pick up someone from the railroad station. Then I travel with him to catch up on East Coast news from the station cats and the latest feline arrivals. And no, I've never felt the urge to go back.

Sylvie and I don't bother with agents or climbing up onto directors' casting couches. We cast ourselves. Whenever a film is shooting, we slip onto the sound stage and see what's going on. We've both got theater training and can tell instinctively when a scene needs a cat; then we simply appear. Most times the director doesn't even know we're there; the continuity girl is usually so busy checking something inconsequential that she doesn't notice either. It is just

as well we always remember exactly where we were in shot, whether our tails were up or down, and precisely what we were doing; the slightest change in position between takes could ruin the film's consistency.

When critics rave about our performances, the way we complete the scene, adding that extra *je ne sais quoi* that raises cinema into art, the once-oblivious directors take all the credit. We don't object. Being true professionals, we are happy if our jobs are well done. We never hog the camera. Cats are not usually central to the action: we simply curl up on a sofa, climb a tree, or saunter down a sidewalk, adding that touch of authenticity that makes all the difference. If you keep your eyes open when you're watching an old movie, you might spot us. These days you could notice one of our youngsters. We've given all our kittens, and their kittens, a rigorous training, much better than they'd get at any acting school. And, of course, they come from generations of dramatic artists, so the skill is in the blood.

THE MOVIE CAT

This cat begins life in Manhattan in the 1930's. He is much more concerned about his theatrical pedigree than any other, but his appearance shows that he is a Maine Coon Cat.

Manhattan, central New York, is an island, set in the Hudson River which divides around it. It is separated by a narrow channel from the Bronx, by the main channel of the Hudson from New Jersey, and by the East River from Brooklyn and Queens. Broadway has always been New York's theater district, especially in the section around Times Square and 42nd Street.

From the 1920s to the 1960s, many theaters were taken over by the big screen; the cinema dominated the entertainment industry.

Centered around the big Hollywood studios to which most of the stars, writers, and directors were contracted, movies were turned out on a production line, following a studio plan rather than being conceived as independent productions as they usually are today. Location filming was rare, as most scenes were shot on an indoor studio set or on a set built on the backlot.

The "Bond" cat; Blofeld's pet in You Only Live Twice.

Breeds

The Maine Coon Cat (above) is an American breed, popular in the nineteenth century, but largely forgotten until the Central Maine Coon Cat Club was established in 1953. A large cat with a long and heavy coat, it has a full ruff and a plume-like tail.

Silver Tabby is one of the most attractive patterns for both the Persian and the American Shorthair Cat. The paler background to the bands or blotches of the pattern is made up of black-tipped hairs which give the same lustrous shimmer as that of the Chinchillas. American Shorthairs, or Domestic Shorthairs as they used to be called, are less square in shape than the British and European Shorthairs. They have a rather oblong head with full cheeks and a square muzzle.

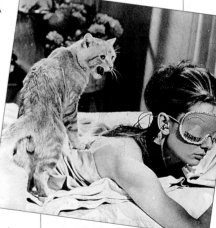

Holly Golightly (Audrey Hepburn) and Cat in Breakfast at Tiffany's.

Starstruck

The movies have created many cartoon cat

characters, but have also provided opportunities for real feline thespians.

Rhubarb provided a great opportunity for a ginger tabby to play a cat which inherited a fortune and a football team. *Breakfast at Tiffany's* gave an unknown crossbreed a chance as Holly Golightly's Cat. And a pretty, fluffy kitten had a cameo role in *La Dolce Vita*. *The Cat From Outer Space* was one of many Disney films to feature cats. Here, the star is Amber, who plays a starship commander whose collar allows her to control and speak to humans when her spaceship lands on earth.

There have been many other less demanding roles in horror movies or as elegant pets and in street-cat character roles which have carried part of the action or add authenticity to a scene.

The field in which cat performers have made their biggest mark is the television commercial, both as an element to emphasize a particular quality of the product sold, and in their own right to advertise cat foods and related products.

It's La Dolce Vita *for this cute kitten.*

Crossing the continent

Purely animal movies in which cats have leading roles have included the *Japanese Adventures of Chatran* (known as *Milo and Otis* and narrated by Dudley Moore in its English-language version) and Walt Disney's *The Incredible Journey,* which

Amber, The Cat From Outer Space.

showed a cat and two dogs finding their way across America. This was not an isolated feat. There are reports of a number of cats finding their way back home across long distances or, even more surprisingly, tracing owners who have moved far away. One, for instance, left Chicago and traced its owner in Boston, Massachusetts, 950 miles away. Another, left behind in California, appeared 14 months later in Oklahoma, while one from New York took five months to reach California. That journey probably did not include a railroad trip, but what is amazing is not so much that a cat could cross an entire continent, but that it knew exactly where to go. It is surely inconceivable that this cat arrived at the precise destination just by chance.

Stage cats

There are cat characters in ballet, opera, English Christmas pantomime, and straight plays, but usually they are portrayed by people who are playing animals. Not one of the parts in *Cats*, the internationally successful musical by Andrew Lloyd Webber and T.S. Eliot, has been played by a real cat! It is not often that a real cat is cast, except in circus or similar acts. A cat, however, though not necessarily seen, is a key participant in the early English play *Gamma Gurton's Needle,* and one of the best cat roles is in John van Druten's *Bell, Book, and Candle* as the familiar of a modern-day witch.

Kim Novak with Pyewacket in the film Bell, Book, and Candle.

In my last life, I am an elegant and highly intelligent Seal Point Siamese living with a successful writer. Her work is not bad, but when she sleeps, I have the opportunity to be creative in my own right. That's when I write my memoirs....

9

THE
LITERARY
CAT

I was at a cat show, trying to sleep and ignore the whole thing when I first met Deskbound. Not until I smelled her friendly perfume did I realize I was being looked at.

I opened my eyes quite slowly. She was there, just looking through the bars of the cage and smiling warmly.

"Hello," she said. I looked at her more carefully.

"What beautiful blue eyes." I blinked them at her and twitched my whiskers. "You're lovely."

Two days later, she visited the house where I was living. As soon as she came in, I bounded across to her.

"Hello! Do you remember me?" she asked.

Of course I did. I left with her that afternoon. I would never recommend that any cat make a decision about a human on such a short acquaintance, but I knew I must not miss this chance. Some instinct told me this was where my future lay and that I would be happy with this human.

The first days in my new home convinced me I was right. Comfortable surroundings, no territorial competition as far as the orchard, bed-rights established straight away, my own magnetic latchkey, and a cute little collar to carry it on. Not to mention good food always served on time, music on the radio that usually matched my tastes, even horse-racing and ballet occasionally on television — my favorite viewing. What more could I ask for?

Well, attention. Though it was not wanting at first. Deskbound doted on me, and in return I taught her all the games I knew. She was quite imaginative at creating new ones as well.

In the early days I was absorbed in exploring my new territory, marking it out and investigating the other residents: frogs by the pool, a squirrel that came visiting, butterflies to catch, and all sorts of creepy crawlies, but there were no other kittens to play with.

As I got older I adjusted to Deskbound's sleep timetable, dozing most of the night and cutting down on daytime naps. This left me with long periods daily when I wanted to play. It was then I began to realize I had a rival for Deskbound's company – that desk.

She had one peculiar toy on the desk that she tapped with her fingers. Little sticks would jump out, marking the paper. I tried to catch the sticks before they hit the roller, but I couldn't. They were very fast, and when they struck my paws they really stung! The roller would move sideways slowly and suddenly move back. A bell rang, presumably to give warning, but it always rang too late for me. Several times when I sat beside this machine I got a biff on the side of the head when the roller bounced back. Once I got so annoyed, I whacked a pile of papers on the floor. Deskbound sighed in desperation and got down on the floor to play with me.

I invented a new game: scrabbling my way under the papers so that she had to find me. Deskbound didn't seem to like that game and irritably picked up all the papers. In fact, she picked me up, too, and put me outside the door, saying, "Please George, I'm trying to work!"

She called me George, despite the fact that I was female, after the famous literary lady of the same name. It was then I decided to call her "Deskbound." I kept off her desk for a while after being put outside, just rubbing against her now and again to invite her to play. She did stop quite often, but one day when she was being particularly workaholic, I tried running up the curtains. She wasn't pleased, but I got her attention. I was so delighted that my concentration lapsed and my claws got caught; I panicked and she had to free me.

"You haven't done any real damage," Deskbound said, "but if you want to rush around, you'd better do it in the yard." She carried me downstairs, put me out, and locked my own door against me!

I was furious and hurt at the same time. Running straight up the tree outside her window, I climbed out along the branch which almost touched the window and meowed violently at her. She looked up, saw me, and shook her head.

The window sill was too far to jump, so I checked the tree for birds' nests – nothing. However, it was quite pleasant up there, so I found a comfortable fork and settled down for a nap. Just as I was dozing off, I had a most peculiar dream – about a tomcat, a handsome tabby. Stranger still, when I woke up there he was, or at least a fellow who looked very like him. The cat was slinking across the end of my backyard. I meowed to indicate he was trespassing. He looked up in response, and I saw he had the most beautiful deep sapphire eyes. Then he disappeared with a flick of his tail. Even so, I still wondered whether I should make a show of chasing him off, just to let him know who was boss?

I decided against it. I thought it might be nice if he came back; someone who might have time for fun and games, perhaps. I could see old Deskbound still sitting on the other side of the window. She looked out, probably hearing my call. To punish her for ignoring me all day, I pretended I was stuck up the tree and gave her a forlorn look. She gave a worried frown and disappeared.

I had climbed too high to jump down or run down the trunk, but knew I would be able to descend backwards. Just then, Deskbound appeared below me with a ladder.

"Oh, poor puss, you have been stuck up there all day and I've ignored you." She made a huge fuss of me and never locked me out again! I was even allowed to sit on the desk once more.

Sometimes Deskbound would spend hours writing with her pen; I tried catching it as it wiggled about and managed to run off with it in my teeth. She laughed as she took the pen from me, but when I jumped up on the desk and tried to do it again, she said, very firmly, "No, George. This isn't a game."

I didn't want to get sent out again, so I put a soft paw on her hand and then gently wiggled the pen with my teeth while she still held it. I could write, too!

"Very clever, George," she said. "I'd love for you to write my books for me, but if I'm going to earn us our dinner, I have to get on."

I didn't mind. My thoughts were wandering to Sapphire Eyes. I trotted down to the yard and gave him a call on the off-chance that he might be around. Amazing! He was there in seconds. He might have been waiting for me.

The tabby was very polite; a newcomer, full of apologies about being in my yard. I told him that, provided he acknowledged the territory was mine, he'd be a welcome visitor. We had a bit of a chase and a game of hide and seek, then his owner called him and he had to go, but promised he'd come again – and suggested I visit him.

We saw quite a lot of each other over the next few days. I cannot pretend that he was highly educated or even very bright, but there was something about him that was very attractive and – well, one thing led to another.

I was worried how old Deskbound would react when it became clear that there were kittens on the way. In fact, she was most understanding and very supportive. Not so the handsome tabby. He didn't lift a paw to help.

The pregnancy all went very smoothly, thank goodness. Tiring in the last week or so, of course. During that time, I was much less mobile; no running up curtains in that condition! I thought the closet might make a good place to retire to, but Deskbound made a box in a warm, draft-free corner of her study. With a bit of re-arrangement on my part, it was really very comfortable, especially when, at the last minute, she moved food and facilities up there, too.

It all happened quite quickly: two males and two females – three looked like me, one male like him. Really, the birth was the easy bit. The hard work came after – well, any cat that has raised her own will tell you – kittens are hell: always hungry and pestering to be fed. The washing and cleaning up after them is neverending: meanwhile having constantly to keep a watchful eye in case they stray off and get into danger or cause trouble.

Oh, yes, I was proud of them. You never saw lovelier kittens. In fact, they were probably less trouble than most. Still, I decided that four was enough for one lifetime. So I had the operation.

I suppose it was my comeuppance for demanding so much attention from Deskbound; but my kittens never stopped pestering me – always demanding to be played with.

"Mom, why don't you flick your tail?"

"Mom, I'm hiding, come and find me!"

"Mom, just pull this piece of string."

"Mom, I've lost my ball, where is it?"

For Bast's sake! They had a brother or sister to play with. Couldn't they give me a moment's peace?

At my instigation, Deskbound found nice new homes for three of my kittens. I decided that the ginger boy should stay with me. He's got a dark patch on his belly, so Deskbound calls him Blot, but I call him Pornphoi – it's a traditional Siamese family name. He's grown up to be quite good company, though still showing proper filial respect – nothing like his father, I'm pleased to add. I'm no longer reliant on Deskbound for games and diversions, though she spends lots of time with both of us.

As Pornphoi got older, he frequently went out exploring by himself, and then I would often take up my old place on the desk, or settle on Deskbound's lap when she was working. I began to take more interest in what she was writing. She sometimes reads me bits aloud, and when she doesn't, I've learned read it for myself.

She put me in one of the latest books. Well, not quite me, but a Siamese that's like me. Soon after that, lots of people came around with bright lights and cameras to film Deskbound reading some passages and to interview us both. She had been nominated for a literary prize.

"And is this animal the original of the feline protagonist?" the pompous interviewer asked. He did not put one question to me directly, but I answered anyway. Not that he seemed to understand. I got annoyed, went over, and batted a pile of manuscript pages onto the floor just to show it. However, he seemed to think this was very amusing and picked me up and stroked me very nicely.

A couple of nights later, we all settled down on the couch to watch "Bookworld" on television. They said the most wonderful things about Deskbound, and there was I sitting on her shoulder. As Deskbound read out some of the best bits, they showed me and Pornphoi playing in the garden. They had filmed that secretly without us knowing!

All the authors on the shortlist for the prize were invited to a big prize-giving banquet, and Deskbound took me with her! The day after the television program a big limousine arrived and drove us to the city. I wore my best suede and diamond collar (no, they're not real ones) and looked out of the window all the way.

We were soon on the main highway and that was rather boring, except for a few views from high hills, and the rows and rows of little houses in the suburbs made me realize how lucky I was to live out in the country, but as we got closer to the city with its tall buildings and elegant facades, it began to get exciting.

We drew to a stop beside a bright red awning and stepped out onto a red carpet with flashbulbs going off all around us. Inside was a high vaulted hall with an orchestra playing and hundreds of people sitting at tables set for dinner. We joined our publisher at one of them. I had my own red plush chair on little gilt legs, and when the food was served, I was given a special dish of shrimp.

After we had eaten, the music stopped and people on a platform started making speeches, saying how hard it was to choose the winner. Then the decisions came. I was so agitated I couldn't stop myself from digging my claws into the chair seat. No, it wasn't us, someone went forward, I couldn't really see them, and everybody clapped. Then they announced the second prize, and then – it was us! Well, third's better than nothing! Deskbound kissed her publisher, gathered me up, and began to pick her way between the tables. Now everyone was cheering, louder than for any of the others. That was when I realized that I had got it wrong. They gave the prizes backwards – we had won!

I had to balance very carefully on her shoulder as Deskbound shook hands with a distinguished gentleman and was handed an envelope, then she lifted me down onto a little lectern, and she made her speech – and told them that I should share her prize because I was the one who had given her inspiration! I positively swelled with pride – for her, of course, not for myself.

I really don't remember much about what happened after that, it was all so overwhelming. When we got home that night, Deskbound told me she had a surprise. She had made a video recording of the award ceremony, and, when she switched the television on, I saw myself sitting proudly on the lectern as

124

she gave her speech of thanks. Watching it, I knew that things could never be quite the same ever again.

Being famous didn't alter Deskbound one bit, but it made me realize how hard she works and why she has to stick at it when Pornphoi and I would like to have her attention.

I decided that I was going to help her. She said she wished we could write her stories for her. Well, at least I'd write my own and give them to her to sell to her publisher. I've got lots of stories in my head – stories about all the cats before me set in past times and exotic locations. I don't know where they come from. Perhaps they were always there; perhaps they come in dreams, maybe I heard them from mother when I was a kitten, or they may be entirely a product of my imagination.

Ideas are no problem, getting them on paper is not so easy. Fortunately Deskbound has got rid of her old "toy," the typewriter she used to write down her stories. Her new machine has keys just like the other, plus a sort of television set that messages come up on as you tap them on the keyboard. I've watched carefully and I know how to operate it. It's quite difficult to hit only one key at a time, but I've slipped off the bed at night and put in hours of practice. I still have trouble switching it on – but Deskbound usually leaves it on all day, even when she goes out shopping, so that's shouldn't be a problem.

Oh, listen, she's going out now. So, if you'll excuse me, I have work to do. I can feel another story coming on.

THE LITERARY CAT

Cats appear in many stories, and numerous poems have been written about them — and Cat Chronicles *is not the first book of which a cat has provided the authorial voice. From the writings of Paul Gallico and Kinnosuke Natsume's* I am a Cat, *to* Love Affairs of an English Cat *by Honoré de Balzac, cats have long played a leading role. One must not forget that queen of alley cats, mehitabel, though Don Marquis used a cockroach called archy to tell the stories. He could only jump on one typewriter key at a time so he never uses capital letters.*

Samuel Johnson, Walter Scott, Charles Dickens, and Henry James were just a few of the international writers all devoted to their cats. Lewis Carroll gave cats a major role in the Alice stories.

And no cat lover would disagree with Mark Twain's comment: "A home without a cat, and a well-fed, well-petted and properly revered cat, may be a perfect home perhaps but how can it prove its title?".

Alice and the Cheshire cat from Alice in Wonderland

Royal cats

Siamese cats probably did come to the West from Siam for, although they are not the most common cat in Thailand and the genetic mutation that creates their distinctive pattern occurs elsewhere, they used to be part of life at the Thai court. Siamese cats were carried in the coronation procession of the kings of Thailand and at a royal funeral were placed in the tomb. There was always a space through which the cat could exit, and when it was seen to emerge, it was considered that the soul of the king had passed into the body of the cat and could then witness the installment of his successor.

The crossed eyes and kinked tail which were once common in Siamese cats have now been bred out in pedigree show cats. They have a distinctive, svelte configuration, and their pale coat has dark markings or "points" on the head, extending over the mask and ears, on the tail and on the paws, extending up the lower legs. Patches of color on the belly, white "spectacles" around the eyes, or dark coloring over the throat or the top of the head would all be faults on the show bench. Siamese kittens are born without apparent color markings, which first appear as a smudge around the nose, developing as they get older.

To the original Seal color (above) have been added Siamese with points in Blue, Chocolate, Lavender (or Lilac, also sometimes

Illustration for
The Cat Who
Walked By Himself
by Rudyard Kipling.

known as Frost), Red, Cream, and in Tortoiseshell and Tabby versions of all these colors – the color and pattern are restricted to the points. Some American registration bodies accept only the first four colors as true Siamese and class the others separately as Colorpoint Shorthairs.

Show time

Cats competing in a show must have their pedigrees registered with the body under whose rules the show is organized and must conform to a breed description, the "standard", laid down by that body. Breeders and judges will try to develop cats and make their assessments according to the way in which they understand and interpret those standards. As each

generation of cats becomes closer to the ideal, it is understandable that interpretation of that ideal becomes more extreme. This can lead to problems.

In the Siamese the standards ask for a long, slender body with slim legs and a well-proportioned head with the width between the eyes narrowing down to a fine muzzle in a straight line. Among cat breeders there developed a growing preference for rather frail-looking animals with a long, tapering, wedge-shaped head with a flat forehead, especially in the United States where the description specified a "dainty" cat. This produced an extreme form in contrast to the sturdier cats of a decade or so ago and quite unlike the much more bulky looking Siamese of the beginning of the century. In the United States, where by 1980 the Siamese had become the most popular of breeds, this led to a disaster, with cats becoming weak genetically and prone to illness. Fortunately, the recognition of the wider range of colors and of tabby and tortoiseshells in Britain helped to prevent the same thing happening there, although a much more extreme look was still created. Happily, some breeders have now begun to return to a preference for the older type.

Homage to cats

Numerous poets have mourned their cats in feline epitaphs, from the tenth-century Arab poet Alalaf Alnaharwany, through Thomas Gray and Thomas Hardy to George MacBeth. Théophile Gautier, Heinrich Heine, Charles Baudelaire, Pierre Loti, Lafacdio Hearn, Stevie Smith, Ted Hughes, and Harold Munro (Saki) are only a few of the poets who have included their cats in their work. Christopher Smart wrote one of the most beautiful evocations of a cat, his pet Jeoffrey, in *Jubilate Agno*, a poem written during confinement in an asylum. Artist and versifier Edward Lear, although not a poet in the same mold, often sketched his cat Foss (above), as well as including cats in his rhymes.

Kipling's cat

The Cat Who Walked By Himself, written in 1902 by Rudyard Kipling, sums up the independence of the cat's nature. It tells how other animals, such as cows, horses, and dogs, were tamed to serve man, but the cat would never be tamed completely: "He will kill mice, and he will be kind to Babies… But when he had done that, and between times, and when the moon gets up and the night comes, he is the Cat who walks by himself."

CREDITS

Quarto Publishing would like to thank the following for providing photographs, and for permission to reproduce copyright material. While every effort has been made to trace and acknowledge all copyright holders, we would like to apologize should there have been any ommisions.

KEY: T = TOP; M = MIDDLE; B = BOTTOM; L = LEFT; R = RIGHT